OLLIE
and the science of
TREASURE
HUNTING
A 14-DAY MYSTERY

ERIN
DIONNE

OLLIE

and the science of

TREASURE
HUNTING

A 14-DAY MYSTERY

DIAL BOOKS FOR YOUNG READERS an imprint of Penguin Group (USA) LLC

TW
Dio

DIAL BOOKS FOR YOUNG READERS
Published by the Penguin Group
Penguin Group (USA) LLC
375 Hudson Street
New York, New York 10014

USA | Canada | UK | Ireland | Australia | New Zealand | India | South Africa | China
penguin.com
A Penguin Random House Company

Library of Congress Cataloging-in-Publication Data

Dionne, Erin, date.
Ollie and the science of treasure hunting : a 14-day mystery / Erin Dionne.
pages   cm
Summary: While spending two weeks at Wilderness Camp on the Boston Harbor Islands,
thirteen-year-old Ollie, short, half Vietnamese, asthmatic, and overweight, must find and protect
hidden pirate treasure from those who would steal it for themselves.
Includes bibliographical references.
ISBN 978-0-8037-3872-0 (hardcover : alk. paper)
[1. Camp—Fiction. 2. Buried treasure—Fiction. 3. Vietnamese Americans—Fiction. 4. Racially mixed people—
Fiction. 5. Mystery and detective stories. 6. Boston Harbor Islands (Mass.)—Fiction.] I. Title.
PZ7.D6216Ol 2014
[Fic]—dc23
2013031211

Printed in the United States of America
1 3 5 7 9 10 8 6 4 2

Designed by Jasmin Rubero
Text set in Adobe Jenson Pro

*For Frank, who is always prepared, and
for Liz, who worked just as hard on this book as I did*

OLLIE
and the science of
TREASURE HUNTING
A 14-DAY MYSTERY

BEFORE

"Stay out of trouble."

Kids hear that all the time, and most of the time we barely pay attention.

But when an FBI agent says it, and it's the fourth time in two weeks that you've been to the federal building in Boston? You listen.

Or try to.

My mom, Agent Goh, and the lawyer who my dad insisted be present after our second trip—but who didn't seem to do anything other than drink more cups of coffee than was humanly possible—were in Conference Room B, the same one I'd been in the other three times I'd been "debriefed." That was a nice way of saying "questioned until I couldn't remember my name anymore."

Agent Goh leaned across the table, his gelled spiky black hair glittering in the overhead light.

"Stay out of trouble for me, okay?" he repeated, but this time with less of an "I'm an FBI agent" serious ring to it and more like the tired way my homeroom teacher last year would say it, when she'd get a headache and pinch the bridge of her nose.

1

"Stay out of trouble, lay low. And have fun." He leaned back in his chair. "Geocache. Hang out by the campfire. Swim." Then he turned his gaze to my mom. "Mrs. Truong, thank you for being so understanding. We believe this is the best course of action for Oliver. It will keep him out of the spotlight and let us wrap up the case against James O'Sullivan."

My mom, whose hands were folded together so tightly the knuckles were white, gave a curt nod, like her neck was wound too tight and it hurt her to move it. "Of course. He loves camp. It just seems so *soon* . . ." She trailed off and took a minute to sweep a stray piece of sandy hair behind her ear. My mom's had the same hairstyle ever since I can remember—and has swept the same piece of hair back forever—but today the gesture revealed how tired she was. And for the four thousandth time since all of this started, I felt bad. I hadn't understood what solving one of the biggest crimes in Boston would do to my family. Everyone was stressed. News vans and reporters had been camped out in front of our house for *days*. This morning, Mom and I had to leave through the back door and cut through our neighbor's yard to get out without them seeing us. My dad had taken two weeks out of work—weeks he'd been saving so we could go to Vietnam and visit my grandmother in the fall. That trip would be rescheduled. Even my little sister, LeeLee, was freaked out. She'd wet the bed three times last week, and she hadn't done that in over a year.

"You're not in any danger, and neither is Ollie," Agent Goh said. "We're confident that Sully and his daughter were working

2

alone. We just need to keep Ollie out of the media spotlight so we can do our jobs. The media glut has been a bit ... distracting."

Their "jobs" were collecting evidence from the three historical landmarks my best friend Moxie and I had broken in to or defaced in our quest to find over $500 million in art stolen from the Isabella Stewart Gardner Museum—which we'd found, and returned, and were each $2.5 million richer because of it. Or we would be, when they finished verifying the paintings' authenticity. But thanks to some guy who worked in the restoration department at the museum and had visions of being a TV star, our names had been splashed all over the media—a "distraction" for the FBI, but miserable for me, Moxie, and our families.

Mom sighed, and I felt lower than a snail's butt. Staying out of trouble had always been pretty easy for me. When you're short, a mix of Caucasian/Vietnamese, asthmatic, overweight, and look a little too much like the kid in that animated movie about the old guy who floats his house away with a zillion balloons, there isn't much trouble to get into. I played video games, geocached, and hung out with my friend Moxie—who was already on her way to New Hampshire with her mom and her mom's boyfriend (that was their solution to the "lay low for a couple of weeks" directive).

My parents couldn't get more time off work, so I'd be heading to Wilderness Scout camp on the Boston Harbor Islands. My troop was scheduled to go in August, but the FBI wouldn't let me wait that long—so I was going with another troop from Boston, with a bunch of guys I didn't know. Not that I cared much. After spending two weeks either dodging reporters or in Conference Room B, I was ready to get outside and away from this stuff.

Staying out of trouble? No problem.

Riiiighhhht. . . .

WILDERNESS SCOUTS TROOP 7

Harbor Islands Camping Trip Roster—July 18–August 1

Mr. J. Fuentes	Scoutmaster
Dr. A. Gupta	Parent volunteer
Derek Symonds	Troop Leader, 17
Steven Washington	Troop Leader, 17
Peter Mallory	16
Doug Spezzano	16
Jorge Vargas	16
Horatio Fuentes	15
Ravi Gupta	15
Cam Przybylowicz	15
Jack Kadleck	14
Manuel Ramierez	14
Christopher Imprezzi	13
Provo Member: Oliver Truong	13

To: All Troop 7 Scouts attending the BHI Camping Trip

From: Scoutmaster Fuentes

Subject: Orienteering Challenge

To kick off our 2 weeks of summer camp, we're beginning with the annual Orienteering Challenge/Scavenger Hunt. Below are a series of coordinates and clues that you must navigate to find our departure point. Our boat leaves promptly at 2 pm; the challenge begins at 1pm.

Good luck!

1 pm: Begin at N42 21.60384 W71 3.37272

- Find the statue of someone named Red. What's he holding?
- Cross the Greenway, but instead of an X, these "rings" mark a spot. How many are there, and what is it?
- Who barks at N42 21 32.87 W71 2 58.79?
- Not a rose, but close! We salute you.
- End coordinates: N42.3564864 W -71.049773

DAY 1

1

Here's how you get into trouble trying to find a boat:

Get there first.

"Not a rose, but close . . . Not a rose, but close . . ." I squinted at the clue again. I was standing just past the New England Aquarium, the sea lions in their outdoor tank barking for more tiny fish from the handlers. The first of Scoutmaster Fuentes's riddles were really easy for me to solve: the Red Aubach statue in Faneuil Hall, the Rings Fountain on the Greenway, and the aquarium's sea lions. But the rose one? This was tough.

I closed my eyes, turned the riddle over in my head:

Not a rose, but close.

Where were there roses in Boston?

That's when I realized I was "distracted by the shiny," as Moxie says. Sometimes, when you're trying to find something, it's actually right in front of you—you just can't see it because you're looking at something else bigger and shinier. The word *rose* was a distraction—the crux of the clue was "We salute you." What do we salute?

The flag.

That was it! There was a giant flag in downtown Boston—at *Rowes* Wharf!

I headed down Atlantic Avenue, the aquarium behind me, dodging tourists and people dressed for work, and soon came to the giant rotunda at the Boston Harbor Hotel. The flag that waved in the wind there was taller than my house.

I stood underneath it and typed the final set of coordinates in my handheld GPS, then took off.

The traffic on Atlantic Avenue struggled past, the cars' exhaust adding to the heat of the morning. I swiped my forearm across my brow—a Wilderness Scout no-no; we were supposed to use a handkerchief when in uniform—but the sweat came right back.

The GPS chimed. I glanced down. Direction shift. East.

I turned left, onto the Harbor Walk—this cool paved path that had been built along Boston's waterfront, behind all the hotels, restaurants, and shops. Moxie and I had plans to walk the whole thing this summer, but that hadn't happened.

Most of our summer plans had recently changed.

The GPS chimed again. North.

I turned. Sweat rolled down my back. I'd have a wet patch there when I took my pack off.

Now the water was to my left, a swanky apartment building was on my right. Sweet boats—so sweet they had decks and wooden trim and, from what I could see through the windows, TVs larger than the one in my house—were docked all along the route.

Would I be getting on one of those?

The GPS arrow started blinking, which was how it signaled that I was approaching the destination coordinates. I looked all around. A big boat—really big, like, it had a *helicopter landing pad* on it—was parked in front of me.

Seriously? Wilderness Scout Troop 7 sprang for a yacht?! No way. Not possible.

I was the first person here.

I stopped in front of the yacht. My GPS was blinking like crazy. This *was* the spot.

I checked my watch: Fifteen minutes to spare.

No Wilderness Scout troop could afford a yacht with a helipad. What the . . . ?

Then, over the lapping of the water came a cross between a bleat and a honk. It sounded like a sick goose.

I walked down the length of the yacht, toward the harbor. A regular harbor islands ferry bobbed in the water. The horn blatted again.

Typical Boston, I thought. It's a fight over a parking space.

A few bleats later, a very sleepy-looking guy appeared on the deck of the yacht. There was some yelling—apparently the slip was supposed to be empty and ready for the island hopper boat we'd be taking—and then the yacht started rumbling and two other guys materialized to untie it.

"Yeah, baby! That makes six years. In. A. Row!" The shout came from behind me, at the head of the pier. I followed the sound.

A tall, lanky kid with sandy hair, an untucked uniform, and a smug expression leaned against one of the concrete pilings, pack at his feet.

"Hey," I said, sticking out my hand. "I'm Ollie."

He shook it, hard. "Derek. Troop leader. I didn't think any other troops were coming on this trip," he said, gesturing to my Troop 5 patch.

"I'm provo with Troop Seven," I explained.

"Oh. Were you dropped off or somethin'?"

"No," I responded, not understanding what he was getting at. Then it clicked: He thought he'd won the orienteering challenge to find the boat. "I got here first," I said, a prickle of anxiety finding its way into my stomach.

His brow furrowed. "Not possible," he said.

"Uh . . . yeah. It was a good course, though—I nearly got tripped up with the Rowes Wharf clue," I said, hoping this wasn't as big a deal as his scowl made it seem to be.

A dark shadow came over Derek's face, and he stepped away from me. Just then, three other uniformed scouts came around the corner and introduced themselves. One, Steve, had a mess of dreadlocks tied at the nape of his neck and a Troop Leader patch sewn onto the pocket of his uniform. The other two guys were high school age too—one, with broad shoulders and close-cropped hair, introduced himself as Pete, and the other, with dark hair and a pierced ear, was Horatio. All three of them looked a little surprised to see me there.

"D?" Troop leader Steve raised his hand in a celebratory high five. "Six years, right?"

Derek turned to me, eyes hard. "Nah," he said. With an eardrum-busting honk, the yacht unmoored and steered out to sea.

12

Everyone stopped. And looked. At me.

My ears turned pink. "Hey. I'm Ollie. I'm provo with you guys."

"Wait—hey. You're THE KID!" Steve pointed at me. "The art kid!"

My mouth went dry. Crud. I'd been counting on the fact that kids don't pay attention to the news in the summer. Wrong assumption. "Uh . . ." I said.

"Seriously. It was you, wasn't it? You found all that art!" He gave my backpack a friendly slap, which sent me staggering forward. The other guys circled, like sharks smelling a kill.

"Well," I tried. Agent Goh had coached me on what to say in this situation—"I can't really talk about that" was his best suggestion, which sounded better in Conference Room B than it did out here. These guys wanted *details*; ones that I seriously wasn't allowed to give.

"What's going on? What happened? Is that our boat? Who's that guy?" A kid shorter than me, with a pack twice his size, showed up at my elbow. He nearly vibrated with intensity. "Derek, you won, right? Six years in a row! I'll never win. I can't seem to follow the directions on the screen—"

One of the other scouts cut him off. "Derek didn't make it. This is Ollie—the kid who found all that art a few weeks ago. He beat him." The new kid offered me a high five, which I wasn't sure if I should accept. I gave a light one in return. Derek seemed downright *sulky*.

"You beat Derek?! He's been first every year since he graduated to full scout level! That's so awesome. You're a detective too! You must be really smart—and good at orienteering and stuff—to take him out. I mean, no one ever does that!" He kept talking, and Derek's scowl got deeper. The other scouts were getting a kick out of it, nudging one another. One of them gestured to me and I caught the words *Dr. Watson*.

Diving into the harbor seemed like a good plan.

I waited for another second. The kid wasn't going to stop talking. So I interrupted and asked his name.

"Chris," he said, and stuck his hand out. "Troop Seven."

"Ollie," I said, shaking his hand. More scouts trickled onto the dock, and Chris proudly told every one of them that I'd beaten Derek in orienteering. At least it changed the subject from how I'd spent my summer vacation so far.

"Hey, Dr. Watson! Help us find the gangplank," troop leader Steve called. "Time to board."

"Lay low," Agent Goh had said.

Or . . . not.

The boat moved far enough into the harbor to put on speed. The engines got louder, and Horatio and Pete, who were leaning against the railing near me, jumped—then ragged on each other for being startled.

"Hey! Hey!" Chris tugged on my sleeve. "Hey! Is that a whale? 'Cause I think it's a whale. Didja see it? See the shadow? Look!" His Wilderness Scout uniform looked a little . . . bulky . . . on him. Did he have padding on under there?

"I don't think it's a whale," I said. "What was the deal back there? With Derek?"

"No! Seriously! Look!" He tugged and pointed again, and, caving, I followed the line of his finger with my eyes—grayish blue water, relatively calm under the blue sky. I spotted the dark shape he was so jazzed over.

"It's not a whale."

"C'mon!"

"Sorry, but it's not a whale," I repeated.

"How do you know, huh?"

"Because . . ." I pointed up. "It's the shadow from that cloud." Chris followed the line of my finger to the puffy white cloud making its lazy way across the sky.

"Oh." The corners of his mouth drooped and his hair even sagged a little.

"It was the right shape and stuff, though," I offered, wanting to cheer him up.

"I know, right? I mean, it totally looked like one. I couldn't believe it." He went on about the cloud whale for another minute, then cut himself off.

"Sorry—you asked me about Derek. He wins orienteering challenges. Like, every year." Chris shrugged. "He takes it really, really seriously. I bet you could guess."

"Seemed that way."

"So, I gotta ask you about the art stuff. Was it crazy? How'd you find it? Did you look for clues? How'd you even get into it?"

Chris's questions washed over me while I thought about how to even begin answering them. It really wasn't my adventure. I was helping Moxie and got caught up in the whole thing.

"He didn't do any of it." Derek was back. Horatio and Pete

moved closer. "According to the paper, his *girl*friend found all the art; he was just in the right place at the right time." He paused, taking a quick glance around at his audience. "What'd you do? Hold her purse the whole time?"

Whoa. I hadn't expected *this*—lots of questions, sure. Some jealousy, maybe. But defending my role? No. I'd done plenty, but how was I going to explain that? How *could* I explain that, when I was under orders not to talk about what happened? My stomach churned; not from the boat.

"I helped plenty," I said, hating the lame way it sounded to my own ears.

"The only thing this guy's found this summer was the boat!" Derek cackled. I cringed, wishing I was good at sharp comebacks.

The guys—Chris, Pete, Horatio, and one or two others who'd wandered over while Derek was messing with me—cracked up. "Oooh, *burn!*" one jeered.

Derek opened his mouth again, but before he could speak the other troop leader came over to us.

"Dude! There you are! I've been looking for you."

"Why didn't you ask Dr. Watson over here to find me?" Derek responded, on a roll. "He could ask someone where I was."

"Don't be a jerk. You're a troop leader, remember?" Steve directed at him. "Derek is a total idiot," he said to me. "But that's beside the point. I have the stickers! And names." A triumphant smile spread across his face.

"Yeah!" Chris and the others cheered. Even Mouthy Derek grinned.

What were they talking about?

"It's Gotcha!" Pete said, catching my confused expression.

"The Gotcha! game?" Steve tried. I shook my head.

"Provo," sneered Derek.

Steve ignored him and pulled a package of round red stickers out of a pocket. "It's easy," he explained. He tore two sheets of red ones in thirds, and handed Derek, Chris, Pete, Horatio, and me each a section dotted with three stickers. "I give you the name of a scout. Tag him with the red sticker to take him out of the game. You get the name of the person he's supposed to tag and his extra red stickers. Get that guy. And so on. Last man standing wins. No playing in camp sessions or in the campsite—we keep it on the down low. Campsite and bonfire are safe zones."

I grinned and stuffed the stickers in my pocket, then picked a folded slip of paper out of Steve's baseball hat. Although our troop doesn't do anything like this, we play some pretty epic games of Manhunt on camping trips.

Besides, I have a knack for finding things—right? This was up my alley. Going provo would work out after all.

"I've been the last man standing for three years in a row," Derek crowed. "And I'm not seeing any new competition."

"Then you need glasses," I snapped, finally putting the right words together. "You're going *down*."

CHRIS'S GOTCHA! ALIVE/TAGGED LIST

STEVE

D-BAG DEREK

ME (CHRIS)

JACK

MANNY

DOUG

PETE

HORATIO

CAM

JORGE

RAVI

OLLIE

LATER THAT DAY
2

Derek and the others shoved off after we got our stickers.

"Gotcha! *is* really awesome," Chris said, vibrating again. "Last year, it came down to Derek and this other kid, a senior, and Derek hid in a tree for *hours* to get him. He even missed lunch and nearly blew the game. He's a jerk, but really good. Last year I kept a list of who got out and who was still in; I'll do that this time too, just so we can see who's left and guess who has who, 'cause you're not really supposed to tell that stuff. But people totally do, especially to the guys in your cabin. Want to be in my cabin?"

I was only half listening to Chris. My brain buzzed from the run-in with Derek. Defending the Gardner stuff every time I saw him would get old, fast. And what was up with the sidekick comments? Had the papers really presented me that way? Like Moxie had done all the work? I mean, she'd had that geometry proof, but . . .

"Hey—space shot." Chris nudged me.

"Sorry."

"'S okay," he said. "Mom says my talking tires people out." He shrugged. "Anyway, want to be in my cabin?"

"Yeah," I said, glad that he'd asked. Chris seemed like a good guy, and I wasn't sure about anyone else.

"How'd you do in last year's Gotcha! game?" I asked, before he let loose another verbal tsunami.

"Oh. Well, uhh, I usually get out pretty early," Chris mumbled. "They say I'm an easy target because I don't shut up—people just follow my voice and find me. Which is true—technically. Not that I'm an easy target, but I do talk a lot . . ."

As Chris went on, I spotted our island, Lovells, getting closer. Despite the start to the trip, excitement bled through me. My family had visited Lovells on our harbor tour a few weeks ago—which felt like last year, so much had happened since then—and I couldn't wait to explore it.

Lovells Island has a pre–World War I fort on it, and the top of the battlement is visible from the water. The beach beyond the dock is white, dotted with lots of rocks. A hill covered with reedy grass comes after the sand, and then the woods starts.

My family's tour guide explained that each of the thirty-four Boston Harbor Islands has its own secrets: pirate treasure on Gallops Island, a ghost on George's Island, Revolutionary War battlements and World War II hospitals on others. Our campsite on Lovells would be near the fort, and before I'd left I'd printed out the Parks Service geocaching sites to check out. I also wanted to leave one or two of my own.

"We're coming in!" The scoutmaster, Mr. Fuentes, ranged around the boat, telling us to grab our packs and get ready.

I slung my pack over my shoulders, knees buckling a little under its weight.

Chris noticed. "Heavy. Mine too."

The list of things we couldn't bring on the trip was fairly short: anything electronic, with the exception of a handheld GPS device and a digital camera. No phones, no DVD players, no gaming devices—nothin'.

However, we made up for the lack of technology with what we *had* to bring: aside from clothes, we had to provide our own snacks—for two weeks!—sleeping bag, towel, swim trunks, bug repellent, camping knife, sunscreen, canteen/water bottle, and other stuff. My bag was as stuffed as my little sister after eating all her Halloween candy.

The boat bumped up against the dock, and a couple of the older scouts—Derek and Steve among them—jumped out to tie it to the cleats.

"Gangplank's down!" Mr. Fuentes called. "Let's do this!"

Chris beelined for the ramp.

I took a deep breath. Hard part of the summer is over, I reminded myself as I stepped onto the wooden planks of the dock. Time to get back to normal.

But as Derek stuck an elbow into my pack, sending me off balance and nearly crashing into the kid next to me, I wasn't so sure.

We hoofed it off the dock and across the beach, where I fought soft sand, hot sun, and a nagging tightness in my lungs. I didn't want to use my inhaler before we even got to the cabins. The wet patch on my back returned.

"Pick it up, scouts!" called one of the other scouts, a tall guy with dark hair. "Let's get there before the sun goes down."

Chris rolled his eyes. "That's Doug. He wants to be a Marine. I think he pretends he's a drill sergeant at boot camp and we're his underling-guys. Too bad he's the klutziest scout ever; no one takes him seriously."

Finally, we crossed into the shade of the trees, and once the walking got easier my lungs stopped feeling like they were two sizes too small. But we traded easier walking for swarms of tiny no-see-ums, which buzzed around my head. I swatted them away, wishing I'd dug out the bug spray while on the boat.

A few minutes later, the trail we were on opened into a clearing.

"Home sweet home!" called Steve. I looked up, expecting to see the wood-framed cabins my troop stayed in when we camped at Fort Dix last year.

"What're those?" I whispered to Chris.

He cocked his head at me. "Our cabins." He spoke slowly and carefully, like I was someone who didn't understand English.

"Those aren't cabins," I began. "They're—" But before I could get the words out, a now-familiar voice cut me off, jeering.

"Aw, Provo, what'd you expect? Room service and the Four Seasons?"

I ignored him. "Forget it," I directed to Chris.

Instead of wooden cabins, olive-colored tents were set up on platforms in three rows of three tents each. The tents would be large enough to sleep four or six kids, and were tall enough to stand in—cabins made of cloth.

Mr. Fuentes called us together. He took his hat off and wiped his forehead with a dark handkerchief. With his shaved head, gold hoop earring, and goatee, he looked like a pirate. Along with everyone else, I dropped my pack at my feet. Immediately, my shoulders thanked me. I did a quick count of the scouts: Derek and Steve, me and Chris, Doug the Klutzy Drill Sergeant, Pete and Horatio, four guys I'd seen on the dock but who stayed in the boat's cabin the whole time, and Ravi Gupta and his dad, the trip's parent volunteer, who worked with my dad at the Brigham hospital. Ravi was older than me—he was going to be a sophomore or junior—but we'd hung out a few times when our families had gotten together. He was okay. It was his dad who suggested I go provo with the troop once everything went down.

Dr. Gupta gave me a slight nod. I nodded back.

"Okay, guys," Mr. Fuentes began. "Grab a tent, unpack your stuff, and meet at the campfire in one hour to get the schedule and dinner. Steve and Derek, our troop leaders, get the tent at the edge of the clearing. No more than four to a tent. Hustle!"

The group broke apart. Chris and I were joined by two of the inside-the-boat kids: a lanky kid named Manny whose glasses were thicker than mine, and a guy with orange hair whose skin was so white it was almost translucent.

"Jack," he said, and stuck out his hand. We shook.

"Over here!" Manny called. He snagged the tent at the far end of the middle row, closest to the woods. We grabbed our packs and headed over.

"Home sweet home," he said, pulling the flap back. "And perfect for sneaking out."

3

What was Manny thinking?

I ducked through the tent flap and into the musty-smelling space I'd be calling home for the next fourteen days.

"Not again, dude!" Chris groaned and tossed his pack at one of the pallets on the floor where we'd spread our sleeping bags.

"Last year, Manny's goal was to beat curfew every night and go for a midnight swim. He nearly did it, but three days before we were supposed to leave, Mr. Fuentes caught him and we ended up having a troop leader bunk with us for the rest of the time.

"A troop leader who snored," he added. While talking, he picked his pack up, tipped it over, shook it, and dumped his stuff on the pallet. A huge wad of clothes plopped out, a giant jar of peanut butter wedged into the middle of it like a birthday candle in a wrinkly cupcake.

"With a fourth in our tent it'll be harder for them to put a troop leader in here without moving someone out," Jack pointed out.

"You're both just bummed I didn't make the record," Manny said. "I'm gonna do it this year! Look." He showed us how the bottom edge of the tent was torn, detached from the base. There was plenty of room for a kid to sneak through the hole. And it was on the side closest to the woods, not the other tents. It'd be easy to get out.

"You in?" Manny asked me.

I shrugged. "I dunno. It's not my thing." Honestly, I am not that great a swimmer, so night escapes to the beach didn't interest me. I freed my sleeping bag from my pack and spread it out, then quickly piled my clothes and gear next to it.

"You don't come, you cover," he said.

"No problem," I answered, ignoring Agent Goh's voice in my head. This wasn't real trouble, this was just camp stuff.

Dr. Gupta stuck his head into the tent.

"Ollie. Chris. Jack," he said, checking us off on a clipboard.

"Manny." He sighed. "Oh, Manny. You're not going to give Mr. Fuentes trouble this year, are you? No escape artist shenanigans, okay?"

"Hey, Doc G. we're cool," Manny said, giving him a cheesy, big-eyed, innocent expression. "I'm reformed."

Dr. Gupta didn't buy it either.

"Glad to hear it," he said dryly. "I'll be watching. Ollie, can you come out here for a moment?"

The guys turned to me. I shrugged.

"Sure."

I slipped out the tent flap. Dr. Gupta stepped a few paces away from the tent, toward the woods. I followed.

"I know you've had a . . . ah . . . *busy* summer thus far," he said. He pointed to the tents, miming that others could hear. I nodded, my stomach crawling with snakes of anxiety. Where

25

was this going? "I just want you to know that I have a cell phone and you can use it if you need to. If any information comes my way, I'll pass it along."

"Um, thanks, sir," I said, uncomfortable. There wasn't any info that I was hoping to hear—other than that the news had moved on to something else.

"Now . . . relax," he said. He smiled and clapped a warm brown hand on my shoulder, giving me a gentle shake. "Enjoy the scenery."

"Sure. Thanks." I stepped away from him and returned to the tent. Camp was supposed to be an escape from this stuff, but I felt just as scrutinized as I had at home.

"I take that as a challenge," Manny was saying to Chris as I entered.

"Son of a—" Jack said. He checked all of the pockets of his empty pack, then shook it out over his sleeping bag like he was hoping something would Harry Potter itself out of there. "Crap. I forgot sunscreen."

"You can use mine," I offered, stepping to my pile of stuff. I had a brand-new bottle. Jack glanced at it.

"Thanks, but see how white I am? I need, like, night in a bottle. SPF thirty doesn't cut it. I'd have to reapply every ten minutes." He sighed.

I shrugged.

"I didn't bring any," Manny said. He held his arms out. "This brown skin don't burn."

"Duh," said Chris to Manny. Then, to Jack, "I have thirty too. Maybe Mr. F. has the good stuff."

Jack shook his head. "I'm gonna roast. And my mom's gonna kill me."

"Scouts!" Derek's voice echoed through our tent. "Move out!"

Jack grabbed Chris's bottle and squirted some sunscreen into his hand, shaking his head and muttering about his mom.

I let the three guys leave before me.

When the tent flap closed behind them, I took a breath.

Not worrying about anything other than sunscreen? Priceless.

DAY 2

CHRIS'S GOTCHA! ALIVE/TAGGED LIST

STEVE

D-BAG DEREK

ME (CHRIS)

JACK

MANNY

DOUG

PETE

HORATIO

CAM

JORGE

RAVI

OLLIE

4

"Let's go, lovelies!"

I groaned. Why did my mom sound like a man?

And why was my bed so uncomfortable?

"Rise and shine! Get up, pack up, and move out!"

That wasn't my mom.

I opened my eyes. Sunlight beamed through a hole in the tent flap. Camp. Right. Mornings have never been my thing.

Besides, waiting for Jack, Manny, and Chris to finish midnight swim numero uno had me on edge for what felt like hours. Even after they came back and collapsed, exhausted, I hadn't relaxed.

Across from me, Jack sat up, sleeping bag still wrapped around him. His orange hair stood in all directions.

"Dude, you look like a rooster!" Chris called out. He was already dressed and zipping his bag. "I don't sleep much," he said, catching my incredulous expression.

Of course not.

I wanted to flop back onto my hard pallet, but I'd signed up for a great morning camp session: Exploring the ruined fort. I shook the stiffness out of my arms and legs, got dressed, and tossed my GPS and some snacks in my pack.

"Don't forget your stickers," Chris whispered, gesturing to the white strip peeking out from yesterday's shorts pocket.

Last night, Jorge, a kid two tents down, had "died," getting tagged on his way to bed after the bonfire. Derek had distracted him while Doug came from the shadows, laughing like a lunatic, and scared him nearly to death. No one had come after any of us.

"Right." I stuck them in today's pocket, grabbed a granola bar, and headed outside.

Mr. Fuentes and Dr. Gupta were organizing the guys into groups. A bunch were going fishing, some were going to work on merit badge requirements in the woods, and Mr. Fuentes was leading the hike to the fort.

Manny went with the fishing group, and Jack opted to work on his plant identification badge to stay in the shade.

Chris and I started down the trail behind Jorge and Cam, his tent-mate, and Pete. Derek was also in our group. Great.

We got to the fort in no time. Huge and made from granite blocks, it looked kinda like a castle. As we assembled at the edge of the trail, a tall, dark-haired guy in a Park Ranger uniform stepped out of a door.

"I'm Ranger Johnson," he began. "Welcome to Lovells Island." He gave us history about the island—it was used as a quarantine station in the 1600s, as a launching point to recover shipwrecks, and in World War II, the US strung nets from its shore to the shore of Gallops Island to capture German submarines.

"How can you catch subs in a net?" Chris asked. "Because I

can't quite see how that would work, unless the nets were really big, but even then, wouldn't the sub pilot guy see them coming?"

Ranger Johnson listened patiently until Chris took a breath.

He explained how it worked—tangling their engines—and told us he was going to take us inside.

We went through the doorway, which was narrow and low, and into the fort itself.

It was dim and cool in there, and smelled like the stone basement at Moxie's house. I immediately had a sneezing fit. Ranger Johnson switched on a flashlight, even though you could still see.

"Over here," he said, "you can see marks etched into the wall that show how many days the fort was active during the war." We crowded closer.

I felt a hard poke in my back.

"Gotcha!" a voice whispered.

Derek. Seriously? I was out? But we weren't even supposed to be playing during sessions!

I spun around to pull the sticker off and hand him mine, and he smirked at me.

"Kidding," he whispered. "Had you going, though."

Ranger Johnson showed us the battery towers, crumbling messes of granite and steel where the US Army propped guns during all the major wars. I immediately decided that I'd need to check them out once Ranger Johnson and Mr. Fuentes were out of the picture.

I also decided that the dark pits were a great place to set up an expert-level orienteering cache. Maybe I could even talk to the ranger about adding a permanent log cache to the ones that the Park Service organized on the islands.

When Ranger Johnson was finished with his tour, we sat under some trees for a Q&A session.

"Before we start," he began, "I need you guys to understand something really, really important about the islands."

"Where can I take a leak?" Pete interrupted. Ranger Johnson pointed into the trees. "That way. Watch out for—" But Pete was already gone.

"As I was saying, most of the islands—and definitely this one and the ones in this cluster—change size and shape depending on the tide. Shoreline that's exposed during low tide will disappear at high tide. This isn't a problem unless you anchor a boat too far out during low tide, or leave a pair of sneakers or personal belongings close to the shore. Be aware of what the water is doing and you'll be fine.

"Anyone have questions?"

"Is it true that the pirate Captain Kidd was on the islands?" Chris—of course—spoke up. I hadn't heard that before, not even on my family's tour a few weeks ago. "Why was he here? Did he steal stuff from Boston ships?" He fired off about a half dozen other questions before Ranger Johnson got his hands up to slow him down.

"Simmer down there, gunpowder," he said. "There are a lot of pirate stories about these islands, actually. They used to hang dead pirates on Nix's Mate, to warn others to turn around before coming in to the harbor. But Captain William Kidd was actually arrested in Boston for piracy in 1699, and sent back to England for trial. Supposedly he hid part of his treasure on one of the islands, and for one hundred fifty years people searched for it. They'll never find it, though."

"Why not?" Chris was leaning so far forward, listening, I thought he was going to tip over. Pete rejoined the group.

"Well, in 1849 two men who were rabbit hunting found a bottle with a letter in it near a train depot. The letter was signed by Kidd, and said that he'd left 'money, jewels, and diamonds' hidden on Conant Island, and it was sent to a friend in New York. People think he was trying to buy his freedom before he was deported."

"So why didn't people find it, if Captain Kidd gave directions to the treasure in the letter?" That was from Derek. "Seems like everyone would be searching for it and it'd be long gone now. Right, Dr. Watson?"

I ignored the barb, but Ranger Johnson raised an eyebrow at us. Then he pointed to the sky. A plane was passing overhead, lights blinking, coming in for a landing at Logan.

"Conant Island became Governor's Island, and Governor's Island became Logan Airport. Urban treasure hunters occasionally still look for Kidd's stuff, but the consensus is that it was swept into the landfill that was used to connect the islands that now make up East Boston."

Everyone was quiet.

"So that's it?" Chris broke the silence again. "I mean, people just gave up?"

"They didn't just 'give up,'" the ranger said, sounding testy. "People looked for hundreds of years. It's *gone*."

"It's not gone if no one's found it," Derek said. "Betcha the Doc here could dig it up. Or—wait—don't you need Mrs. Watson to help you find stuff?"

"Knock it *off*, DB," I muttered.

Did Ranger Johnson *peer* at me? His eyes were narrowed and his forehead creased. Had he recognized me from the news?

"It's just a story," the ranger finished. "There are lots of stories about the islands."

"So Kidd's treasure's missing. Fine. What about the island to the right of this one?" This time it was Cam who spoke. "The one we can see from the beach? Anything cool about that one?"

"Gallops. It's not open to the public," the ranger explained. "Asbestos issues. People can't go there."

"Like that would be a problem if you're outside," Derek snorted. Behind him, Pete squirmed and scratched at his hands.

"I thought I heard about pirate treasure *there*," I said, remembering the tour I'd taken with my family. "Did the tour guide confuse that with Captain Kidd's treasure?"

Ranger Johnson stayed silent for a moment, like he was trying to decide how to respond. "Do I know you?" he said to me, instead of answering the question.

"Uh . . . no," I said. Chris nudged me.

"C'mon! Ranger, you totally know him! Picture him in black and white, with that FBI agent next to him and his friend."

Surprise and recognition collided on the ranger's face. "The art!" he said. "You found the art!"

"His girlfriend found it," Derek muttered from behind me. Ranger Johnson ignored him, and instead crowed about how he *knew* he'd seen me before. My ears burned, and even Mr. Fuentes looked uncomfortable. Weirdly, so did Pete.

"Well, about that other treasure," he said, finally moving on to something else, "it's not Captain Kidd's. Another pirate, Long Ben Avery, hid diamonds on that island. They've never been found. But I bet no one like *you* has ever looked for them!" He laughed a weird laugh, somewhere between a chuckle and a snort.

"Okay guys," Mr. Fuentes said, clearly thinking it was time to move on, "let's head back for lunch."

"Horatio is dead," Chris whispered when the tent flap closed behind him. I was glad to have something else to talk about other than Ranger Johnson's weird reaction to finding out how I spent my summer vacation. Chris and I had rehashed for Manny and Jack.

"Who did it?" Jack asked.

"Cam, the big kid with the Sox jersey, got him as he was coming back from dinner, right before cleanup," Chris went on.

"Bummer," I said.

"Yeah." Chris launched into the details of Horatio's attack, and I listened pretty carefully. I had to learn how this game was played.

"They totally ambushed him," Chris said. "Horatio had to take a leak, and when he left the campsite and stepped into the dark, Cam, Jorge, and Ravi followed him. Evidently Jorge and Ravi came up behind him after he'd unzipped and they made some bear noise or something—I don't know exactly what they did, but it probably made him pee on his shoe, 'cause he was carrying them when he came back—and when he turned around to see what made the noise, Cam came at him from the side. Good tactic, but a rough night for the dude."

I nodded, running over the scene in my head.

"You figured out how you're gonna get your guy yet?" Jack asked me. He munched an apple while he talked, white bits of fruit spraying from his mouth. So far, he'd managed to avoid the sun like a vampire.

"Not yet," I admitted. I fished the scrap of paper that I'd pulled out of the damp baseball hat from my pocket. "I have Pete."

"Petey's a good guy," Manny said. He flicked his flashlight on and off in our faces, one at a time. "An okay player. He's a junior this year. I think he's in one of the far cabins." He gestured vaguely. "You can take him. I've got Steve. He's gonna be tough, 'cause he's always with Derek."

"But Pete's off limits for a while," Jack said.

"Huh?" That was from Manny.

"Didn'tcha hear? Poison ivy. All over his hands. Guess he got it when he took a leak or something. It's pretty bad," Jack said. He'd seen Pete with Mr. Fuentes after dinner.

"Must've happened when he left the fort," Chris said. "That's what the ranger was going to tell him—look out for poison ivy! Dude, that sucks. I need to work on plant identification so it doesn't happen to me. Anyway, I wonder who *has* me?" He stood still, but vibrated faintly—just getting revved up. "I mean, this is the longest I've ever been alive. Usually I'm taken out right away, and now I'm starting to get nervous, like—is someone after me? I keep expecting someone to jump out from behind a door or get me when I least expect it. But if I'm always expecting it, how can there be a 'least expecting'? So maybe I'll win—" The rolled-up sweatshirt Jack hucked at him caught Chris right in the side of the head. Chris was so surprised, he was quiet for a second. Then he laughed like crazy, and threw the sweatshirt back at Jack. Who chucked it at Manny, who fired it at me. Soon, we were all cracking up and the sweatshirt was bulleting around the little space.

"Hey," I said, hurling the sweatshirt at Jack, "what happens when you get someone in your tent? There's no way to avoid that, right?"

It was like I'd thrown a bucket of water instead of an article of clothing. Everyone stopped; Jack dropped his arm. Game over.

"Well, no," he began. He looked to the other guys for help.

"You don't take out a friend," Manny said. "It's like unwritten law."

"So what do you do?" I asked. "There are only twelve guys here—and they're sleeping in four of the tents. It has to happen." I didn't get what the big deal was; it was a game.

Manny slid his eyes to Chris. "You're not supposed to switch targets," he mumbled.

"So you're just supposed to tag them?" I asked. I didn't see where this was going.

Chris shook his head. "You could, but that's like sacrilegious. People get really ticked. Friendship-ending ticked. 'Cause if you can't trust your tent-mate, who do you trust?"

"So you . . . what?" I still didn't get it.

"You take yourself out," Manny said firmly. "Game over."

DAY 3

CHRIS'S GOTCHA! ALIVE/TAGGED LIST

STEVE

D-BAG DEREK

ME (CHRIS)

JACK

MANNY

DOUG

PETE

~~HORATIO~~

CAM

~~JORGE~~

RAVI

OLLIE

5

Minus DB's and the ranger's attitudes, I had almost shaken off the pre-camp craziness. I'd even gone swimming earlier in the day. But walking to the fort for a bonfire, in the dark, with someone out to get me? Not a recipe to calm my nerves.

Every crackle and crunch of our sneakers on the path seemed extra-loud. Chris was quiet for once, which made it worse.

Manny nudged me and I jumped.

"Dude, you breathe like my grandmother's fat Chihuahua. What's up with that?"

"Asthma." I shrugged.

"Can hear you coming from Boston," muttered Jack. Our flashlights bobbed along the path. Every so often, one of us would shine it at a tree or shadow to make sure it wasn't someone lying in wait. It'd been a quiet Gotcha! day, which added to our stressed-out state.

"It's not like I'm auditioning to be a ninja or anything."

"You should be, if you want to win the game." Chris was back on line. "I mean, Ollie, you've like, avoided bad guys for real! You could totally do it. It'd be awesome if one of us won. We could even help, once we get taken out."

"Isn't that against the rules?" I asked, but what I was thinking was, *Are you guys crazy? Running for your life is nothing like a game!*

Running for your life *is* nothing like a game. Maybe I *could* win? Would that get Derek off my back, or just make things even worse?

"Distraction is always in play," Jack said, shining his flashlight on a crazy grin.

We came into the clearing next to the fort. Doug, Ravi, and Cam were helping Mr. Fuentes build a fire pit—stacking rocks, piling branches—and other guys were hauling arms full of dry kindling from the woods. I grabbed a few short branches and brought them to the pile.

"What troop showed *you* how to make a fire?" sneered Derek. "These won't burn. They're too wet."

I looked down at the sticks in my hands—they were borderline crumbly, they were so dry. Seriously, he was going to play it this way?

"They're fine," I answered, hoping that maybe he was making an honest mistake—it was dark out, after all.

"Yeah . . . Fine if you want to smoke us out. Amateur." Horatio and Pete, hands bundled in bandages, stared at me. Steaming, I dropped my sticks and went to the logs we were using as benches—where I immediately started sneezing.

Crud. I hadn't taken my allergy meds, and the dust kicked up from the dry wood felt like it took up residence in my nose. I sneezed six times in a row, eyes watering and head filling like a fire hose was attached to my sinuses. I fished in my pocked for a handkerchief, blew some mega snot, and hoped it was over—but the sneezes started up again. Everyone stopped.

"Are you okay?" Mr. Fuentes was at my side. The bonfire-building was on hold because of my nasal passages.

"Fine," I said, my voice clotted with phlegm. I cleared my throat, hoping I could get a sentence out before the sneezing kicked up again. "Forgot my allergy meds. I'll go get them." Before he could say anything, I was walking as fast as I could toward the path. The sneezes returned. There were so many, so quickly, they *hurt*.

Camp rules are that you never go anywhere alone, especially after dark, but I didn't care. I didn't even care if I got tagged right then. I just needed to put some distance between me and that bonfire. Maybe by the time I got back, everyone would be so focused on the fire they wouldn't notice me.

The sneezing finally stopped. My head felt full of runny Jell-O, and no matter how many times I blew my nose into my handkerchief, it clogged right back up. I reached my tent, found my allergy pills, and dry-swallowed one. I'd left my water bottle at the fire. A bitter, gritty taste coated my mouth. I blew my nose again and hit my inhaler.

I took my time leaving my tent. Although the meds hadn't kicked in yet, just being away from the wood dust made a huge difference.

When I finally stepped into the night, I was surprised at how quiet it was. I let my eyes adjust to the darkness for the short walk to the fort.

Trees dotted the campsite. I wove between the tents to

the edge of the clearing and across the access road to the fort. Although I was too far inland to hear the waves, there were still plenty of other sounds: rustling wind through the trees, the squawk of a seabird that was up too late, and the garbled shouts and laughter of the guys at the bonfire.

A bright flashlight clicked on. The white light stung my eyes. I squinted and brought a hand up to my face.

"Oliver! That's your name, right?"

It was that ranger, from the fort. Ranger Johnson. He stepped closer. I stepped back, blinded.

"Yes, sir," I said. "Um, it's kind of hard to . . ."

He swung the flashlight away from my face. Green-purple spots fluttered in my vision. I squinched my eyes and rubbed them under my glasses.

"Sorry, buddy. Hey—I was hoping I could talk to you about the Gardner case. Well, not really that, but kind of."

What?

"Um . . . okay," I said. "But I need to get back to the fire pretty soon."

"I'll walk with you. You have a light?" He pointed his at the path, stabbing the dark like it was out to get him. I didn't turn mine on.

"So, you found that stuff, huh?"

I shrugged. "Yeah, I guess." I waited. Everyone wanted details. Details that, according to the FBI, I couldn't give—and really, I didn't want to. This seemed weird.

"I'm interested in . . . finding things too," he went on, I guess when he realized I wasn't going to say more. "As a matter of fact,

I'm working on a project on one of the islands and could use someone of your . . . caliber . . . to help me with it. Would you be interested?"

I had no idea what he was talking about. A project? The orange-yellow glow of the bonfire appeared through the trees ahead of us. I walked a little quicker.

"So?" he prompted.

"I'm not sure what type of project you're doing," I said. "I guess I'd need to know more." I hoped that answer would be enough to send him on his way.

He stopped. We weren't that far from the clearing, and I just wanted to get there and make s'mores and do stupid campfire skits and other, *regular*, scout stuff. A stick cracked to my right. Was someone else out here? The hair on the back of my neck stood up.

Ranger Johnson clicked off his flashlight. A dark curtain blanketed the woods; the light from the bonfire was tantalizingly close.

"Of course you do," he said. "It's about treasure, Ollie. Pirate treasure, to be exact. And I need someone else to help me find it."

Great. Everyone seems to think I'm Indiana Jones now. I was both flattered and exhausted by the prospect. But before I could answer Ranger Johnson, someone else did.

"Then why're you asking him?"

Derek, muscling in where he's not wanted. As usual.

Ranger Johnson clicked his light on, spearing Derek with it.

"What'd you hear, son?" he asked, his voice rumbling like a bear's. Derek shrugged.

"You're looking for something and want this dwee—kid—to help you. But seriously, he didn't do anything to find that art. I read all the articles. It was his girlfriend or whoever. You need something found, I'm the scout to do it."

Not even a minute ago, I wanted to make a break for the bonfire and ditch whatever Ranger Johnson had in mind. Now? I'd find an ice cube in Antarctica if I had to.

"I'll help you, sir," I said, forcing my voice to stay even.

"Me too," Derek added, his words tumbling over mine.

Ranger Johnson stepped away from me and rubbed his chin like he was considering both of us.

"Fine," he said. "I can use two of you. But," he added, "this is strictly between us."

Here's how you get in trouble at scout camp:

Agree to do something before you know what it is you're doing.

6

Ranger Johnson said he'd find us the next day and give us details. Derek rattled off his camp schedule, giving the ranger a series of times when he'd be available. I rolled my eyes and didn't say anything.

Then the three of us walked into the clearing together like we weren't conspiring, like Derek and I got along, like this summer hadn't taken another weird turn.

Despite my allergies and asthma, my favorite smell is a fire. Dad and I build them in the fireplace for mom almost every night during the winter after LeeLee goes to bed. I love how the smell gets into my clothes. I took a deep breath—and sneezed.

"Ollie's back!" Chris called.

"Remember: Between us," Ranger Johnson said. He clapped a hand on my shoulder like he owned me, then let me go. I shrugged off this sinking feeling in my stomach. Or tried to, anyway. I focused on what I knew: I'd be looking for pirate treasure! Who cared if it was on the down low, right?

Derek and I split up and went to our respective logs to sit with the rest of the group, while Ranger Johnson, Dr. Gupta, and Mr. Fuentes stood at the edge of the fire clearing, talking in low voices.

"Why'd you do that, man?" Manny asked. He elbowed me

in the side. "Took you so long to get back that Mr. Fuentes got ticked and sent DB to find you."

I shrugged. The more I kept my mouth shut, the more I stayed out of trouble.

"The asthma, right, Ollie?" Chris went off, blabbing about how his cousin had it and he had to use an inhaler and being around fires made him have an attack. Jack handed me the bag of marshmallows that was going around the circle and I grabbed two. Chris, who hadn't stopped talking—his cousin had an asthma attack at their house one Christmas (triggered by their tree) and had to go to the emergency room—handed me a long stick that he'd been using to roast his marshmallows. I threaded mine and held them over the fire, working on the perfect caramel color on the outside that leads to a gooey center, while, across from me, Doug managed to light the leg of his shorts on fire with a flaming marshmallow. Pete beat it out with his bandages.

When things settled down, Ranger Johnson and the other two adults came to the circle and told the typical campfire ghost stories—the hook hand, the babysitter and killer in the house, and the scout troop that went missing in Yellowstone. Ones we'd heard a thousand times before.

"Are you going to tell them about the Lady in Black?" Dr. Gupta asked. Ranger Johnson didn't answer right away—he made another s'more and ate it slowly, like he was considering the question.

"What's that story about?" Chris asked, mouth full. He sprayed graham cracker crumbs everywhere.

Mr. Fuentes poked at the fire, which was burning low. "It's a local story," he answered.

Ranger Johnson finished his s'more and wiped his hands on his handkerchief.

"It takes place right over there," he said, pointing into the woods. "On George's Island. The island is haunted."

"Sure," Cam said. He stuffed a triple-decker s'more into his mouth. "Ghosts aren't real."

"That's what people say"—Ranger Johnson nodded, indulging Cam—"but I live on that island, and my daughter and I have both seen the Lady in Black." He leaned back, letting the explosion of "no way!" and "tell us!" bounce around the clearing.

He settled in and stirred the fire. The story was about a man who was imprisoned on the island during the Revolutionary War. His wife dressed as a man and tried to break him and his fellow inmates out—and nearly succeeded—but she was captured, tried, and hanged. On the island.

"She still walks the ruined fort, sometimes carrying a lantern, looking for her lost husband," he finished. The fire was down to embers.

"Good story," Ravi said, "but c'mon, you haven't really seen her."

"I have. Twice," he said. "Once when I was fixing a shutter on our house during a storm—I saw a figure holding the lantern in the window of the fort, which is up the hill from our house, and the second time . . . well, that's a story I can't tell right now." The guys groaned and tried to get him to tell more, but the ranger would have none of it.

"I can't," he said. "Really. It scared the heck out of me and I don't like to think of it at night. Seriously."

The other guys begged. Finally, Mr. Fuentes held his hands up. "The man doesn't want to tell the story," he said. "Enough!"

He and Dr. Gupta exchanged glances. They were pulling our leg. I'd heard the story of the Lady in Black before, sure, but I was willing to bet they were staging the "Park Ranger sees a Ghost and Won't Talk About It" part for us.

"Someone *else* must have a story to tell. About something real-life and scary." Steve's voice broke through the disappointed sounds from the troop.

"Ollie! Hey, Ollie! C'mon! Tell us your story!" Chris turned to me. I cringed. I'd look like a jerk for backing out when put on the spot, but I had to.

"Yeah, Ollie!" "Tell us!" the guys pressed.

I shook my head. "I can't," I said. "I'll get in trouble." How was I going to get out of this? And how was I going to kill Chris later?

"Who's gonna tell?" Derek said, suddenly serious and supportive. "Any of you gonna tell?"

The rest of the troop shook their heads. Doug crossed his heart—and eyes. Steve had his HeHeHigh Screaming Hellcats T-shirt on, and he drew an X over the mascot. Ravi and Horatio threw the Wilderness Scout salute and oath. Pete waved his (blackened) bandaged hands.

I turned to Dr. Gupta, hoping he could read my desperation. I knew that the story would be safe while we were on the island, but after having been burned once by someone running to the

49

media, I wasn't about to gift anyone else with that opportunity once we got home.

"Wuss!" "Tell us!" The guys nudged one another and kept badgering me. For the first time since getting on the boat, I realized how alone I was here—some of these guys seemed cool, but I didn't *really* know them. And now they were looking less like camping buddies and more like how I imagined those kids from *Lord of the Flies* looked when things got hinky—big-eyed and a little too excited.

I gulped. Dr. Gupta seemed oblivious to my problem (or maybe he wanted to hear the story too, I thought). I was on my own.

Maybe there was *something* I could tell them? Something that had been in the papers, that Agent Goh wouldn't get angry with me for revealing? I racked my brain.

"Uh . . ." I said, stalling. The guys leaned in, went silent. Someone stoked the fire.

But before I could come up with anything, an eardrum-splitting scream came from the woods.

And then it came again.

7

Everyone froze. I scanned the logs: All of the scouts were here at the circle, as were the three adults. My heart pounded like it did when I'd had the worst asthma attack of my life.

No one else was supposed to be on the island. Who else—or what else—would be here?

The screaming stopped. The silence was worse.

Steve and Ranger Johnson were the first to react. They jumped up—they were almost the same height. Ranger Johnson's face was the dirty white of old snow.

"Hey!" he yelled.

"Where'd it come from?" yelled Steve. A bunch of us, finally able to move, pointed west, behind the fort.

Steve shook Derek's shoulder and the two of them bolted behind Ranger Johnson, around the corner of the fort.

"Stay calm, guys," Mr. Fuentes said, but he looked scared too. "I'm sure it's fine. It's probably—"

The scream came again. Lung-busting, high-pitched, putting LeeLee's tantrums to shame, but this time it sounded like the screamer had moved—like it was coming from the other side of the campfire.

It died out in a wet gurgle. I wanted to throw up.

Chris and Manny pressed against me like bookends.

"Stay here," Mr. Fuentes ordered. "Watch them," he added to Dr. Gupta. He nodded. He was holding Ravi's hand.

"Help is coming! Stay where you are!" Mr. Fuentes shouted. He stepped out of the bonfire circle toward the sound of the scream.

"I'm goin' too." Cam stood and tugged on Jorge's T-shirt. Chris had been silent since the screaming began.

"No way, dude," Jorge said. Cam called him a name. Jorge stood.

The fire was down to embers again; everyone's face glowed orange with deep shadow. My mouth was as dry as the bottom of my shoe.

Cam and Jorge took off after Mr. Fuentes, ignoring Dr. Gupta's orders to come back and sit down.

Bushes rustled and twigs snapped from the direction of the fort. Ranger Johnson and the guys burst back into the clearing, breathing hard.

The scream came again, this time closer, and from yet another spot. Ranger Johnson, Derek, and Steve headed in the new direction, fanning into the woods at three points, so as not to miss whatever was making the sound.

Another short scream and a muffled curse came from the woods.

"They got it?" Chris whispered. I didn't think he knew how to whisper.

"Hope so," I whispered back.

Derek came back to the fire first, smirking. Then Steve, brushing his T-shirt off. Then Mr. Fuentes, shaking his head, and Cam and Jorge, looking ticked.

Last came Ranger Johnson, hand clamped firmly around the upper arm of a skinny blond girl who was grinning like she'd just caught the biggest fish in the lake.

"Boys, meet Grey. My daughter."

Grey wriggled out of her dad's grip. "Gotcha!" she crowed.

"That girl made all that noise?" Manny said. He whistled low, through his teeth. "Not possible."

"I have a sister," I responded. "Totally possible."

Mr. Fuentes and Dr. Gupta told us to clear out and head back to our tents. They'd had enough of us for the night.

As Chris and I crossed the clearing, Grey sidled up next to me.

"You're the kid that found the missing art," she said. She smelled like grapefruit and the ocean.

I shrugged. "So?"

"So that's cool," she said. "But I bet you can't find me."

"I'm not looking for you," I pointed out. "And after that display, I'm not sure I want to."

"Yeah," Chris piped in, "what would he want with you, anyway? You totally creeped us out, and it was an awesome prank, but dude—you totally creeped us out!"

Grey ignored Chris. "We'll see. I'll find you," she directed at me.

"Can't wait," I muttered. What the heck did she want with

me? Did it have anything to do with the pirate treasure that the ranger wanted to talk to me about?

"Grey!" her dad called, and she turned away from us. Chris made a face.

"What was that about?" he asked.

"Trouble," I answered.

DAY 4

CHRIS'S GOTCHA! ALIVE/TAGGED LIST

STEVE

D-BAG DEREK

ME (CHRIS)

JACK

MANNY

DOUG

PETE

~~HORATIO~~

CAM

~~JORGE~~

RAVI

OLLIE

8

Jack woke our whole tent the next morning before sunrise.

"Shhh!" he whispered, after poking me and shaking my sleeping bag. "Keep quiet and hurry up. I gotta show you something." Chris and Manny were already up, bumbling around, throwing clothes on. Manny, three for three on his swims, must've barely slept. Chris was biting his lower lip to keep from talking.

"This better be good," I growled. I rubbed my face, threw on the smoky T-shirt I'd been wearing the night before, and followed the guys out the tent flap.

We crept past the other tents—snores coming from a few of them—in the flat, gray predawn light and entered the woods. A few hundred feet from camp, Jack turned to us.

"So I woke up because I had to take a leak, and then I was up, so decided to take a walk. Wait'll you see this. I hope they're still there." He picked up speed. I glanced at Manny and Chris. Both of them shrugged. They didn't know what was going on either. We got to the fort, but Jack kept going. He was headed to North Beach.

We came out at the top of the dunes. The beach sand was like a white blanket that met the edge of the tall sea grass. Straight across from us, night still hung on. The sky was deep indigo and a few stars still glittered. To our right, due east, the top of the sun was coming over the horizon. Gold and pink light pushed at the sky.

It was pretty and all, but the inside of my sleeping bag was way better.

As I was about to explain that to Jack, he pointed.

"They're still here!"

Manny, Chris, and I turned.

A bunch of porpoises—little ones that live in the harbor and you see playing in boats' wakes—were partying just off the beach: jumping, flipping around, splashing and boiling the calm ocean.

"Whoa," said Chris.

"Dude," said Manny.

"Amazeballs, right?" Jack grinned.

The porpoises played as the sun came up behind them, like they knew this was the only time they'd have the harbor to themselves. One even did that "dance on the tail" trick that you see in aquarium shows.

We didn't speak, just watched.

Definitely amazeballs.

We stayed there until the sun was over the horizon, when the animals headed off to catch fish or do whatever porpoises do during the day. We'd sat on top of the dune in silence except to point out a particularly cool move or big splash.

I brushed sand off my butt and stretched.

"Breakfast?" I asked as we walked back.

Chris nodded. "Dude, I'm starving. And I have water safety this morning. Is that thing about not swimming after eating really true? 'Cause I want to eat, like, a dozen eggs but I don't wanna be the guy that needs rescuing . . ." He kept talking as we passed the fort. A kid in a Red Sox T-shirt jumped out from behind a tree, right at us.

"Run!" yelled Manny. I took off behind him and Jack. Who was the assassin after?

Behind me came a thump, "Oof!" and a triumphant "Gotcha!"

I hit the brakes and turned around. Chris was on his stomach, sand everywhere. The kid who'd tackled him was sitting, hands hanging over his knees, head down, taking deep breaths.

He raised his head: It was Cam, who'd taken out Horatio. He opened his palm.

"Hand over your target and stickers," he said.

Chris knelt and scrubbed his hair with both hands. White sand flitted like snow.

"You nearly killed me," Chris grumbled. He pulled the strip of stickers from his pocket and handed them to Cam along with the slip of paper with his target on it. He tilted his head from side to side, stretching his neck.

"Sorry, dude. I didn't know how fast you were."

"Not very." Chris stood.

"You okay?" I asked. He nodded. Cam left for the campsite at a slow jog.

"Yeah. And now I don't care what the swimming deal is. I'm having eggs." He paused. "And I'm totally going to help one of you guys win."

LATER, DAY 4

CHRIS'S GOTCHA! ALIVE/TAGGED LIST

STEVE

D-BAG DEREK

~~ME (CHRIS)~~

JACK

MANNY

DOUG

PETE

~~HORATIO~~

CAM

~~JORGE~~

RAVI

OLLIE

9

"How are you so good at this?" Ravi grumbled as we trekked through the woods around the fort in an orienteering session, refreshing our navigation skills. "I can never find the stupid end marker."

I swatted some no-see-ums. "It's all straight lines." Orienteering is reading a compass—you get coordinates, have a starting point, and you have to find a specific spot using landmarks and counting steps. "The GPS makes it easy."

"For you, maybe." Ravi tapped his screen. "Mine always says I'm off."

"'Cause you are," I pointed out. I consulted the needle compass in my hand. "We need to go north-northeast." Most of the time when I cached, I used a portable GPS, but I like both methods. And my straight-up compass reading was rusty.

Ravi sighed and pivoted to the right. His device gave a satisfied beep.

"So are you annoyed that my dad keeps checking in with you? I can tell him to lay off." Dr. Gupta had pulled me aside twice more since our initial talk outside of my tent—both times just seeing if I was okay.

I hadn't realized anyone noticed. "It's fine. I think he and Mr. Fuentes want to make sure I'm not going to freak out at the bonfire or something." The joke was lame, but hopefully Ravi would take the hint. The guys had let up about asking me about the heist—for now—but I couldn't avoid the inevitable.

"Okay," muttered Ravi.

"Hey—there's our marker!" The site was a tree with a red flag tied to it.

"Sweet. I'm outta here." Ravi jotted the coordinates on his orienteering badge sheet. I cosigned it as his partner. "Ya coming?"

"Nah. I'm going to chart it."

"Cool." Ravi turned in a slow circle. "Um, which way to the path?" he asked. I almost gave him the coordinates to navigate his way back, but he probably wouldn't have appreciated the joke.

Once he was gone I mapped the site out in my notebook and retraced my route.

I was counting steps to a crooked oak tree that I'd used as a marker, head down to record the distance, when I tripped over an exposed root, and the book—and my compass, which I'd been holding in my free hand—went flying. My glasses also popped off.

"Crap!" I cried. I scrabbled to my knees, hands groping for my glasses like what's-her-name on *Scooby-Doo*, when a girl's voice said: "Hey, looking for these?"

Here's how you get in trouble finding your glasses:

Grey shows up and finds them first.

* * *

I turned and took my glasses from her outstretched hand. Her fuzzy figure came into focus: blond hair, stormy eyes, and shorts and a pink Red Sox T-shirt. Same "I just caught the biggest fish" grin I'd seen on her after she scared the daylights out of the troop.

"Thanks," I said. "Um, how did you get here?"

She pointed through the woods toward the fort. "I walked. From there."

Stupid question, Ollie. My ears burned. I hate it when I blush. Since I'm half Vietnamese, my face doesn't get beet red like Moxie's or Jack's, but my ears turn bright pink instead. And that's not better.

"Um, are you okay?" she asked. Was she mimicking me, repeating the *um?* "Do you need help?"

It probably looked that way. I was still on my hands and knees on the ground.

"Fine, I'm totally fine," I said, and scrambled to stand and brush off. I got that whiff of grapefruit and ocean again.

"What are you looking for now?" She flipped her ponytail over her shoulder, like the girls do at school when they try to get guys to do something for them. I ignored the ponytail.

"A tree," I said. "I found it."

"Oooh, a *tree,*" she mocked. "Challenging."

"I need to get my stuff," I said. I picked up my notebook.

"Want help?"

I didn't answer, just started scouring the ground for my compass. So did she. After a minute, Grey called "Hah!" and raised it, victorious.

"Thanks," I said. "What are you doing out here, anyway?"

"Scoping out the rest of the team," she replied. "And I'm not impressed."

"Team? For what?" This girl was crazy. Unless . . .

"Does this have anything to do with something your dad mentioned?"

She smiled and threw her arms out wide. "Ladies and gentlemen, we have a winner!" she crowed. Before I could get another word out, a whistle tweeted, signaling the end of morning sessions.

"Guess we'll have to finish this conversation another time," she said.

Before my brain and mouth could activate, she was in the trees, heading in the opposite direction from where I needed to go.

"Hey!" I blurted to the retreating pink T-shirt.

She raised her hand without turning around. "We'll talk later!"

Han Solo would say "I got a bad feeling about this." I did too.

Later, I sat with my back to the base of a tree at the edge of camp, notebook propped on my knees, gridding out a cache to hide. I'd drawn a rough map and needed to decide where to conceal the cache.

I counted squares and tried to sketch the fort, but I couldn't get the proportions right. At home, an online map helped, but in this techno-wasteland, I was on my own.

Frustrated, I turned my pencil over and scrabbled at the page. As I did so, an image flashed through my head of Moxie at the Gardner Museum, hunched over and scribbling on her proof as we tried to figure out what happened to the paintings. I almost grinned.

But right after that image, I remembered the running and the dark and the guns . . . and then I didn't feel like grinning at all.

I hoped Moxie was enjoying New Hampshire with her mom and her mom's boyfriend, Richard. He was also a park ranger. Did Ranger Johnson know him? Did Grey?

Then I started thinking about the pirate treasure, and what Grey wanted to talk about.

This was no good. I couldn't concentrate. I tucked my pencil in the book, closed my eyes, and took a few breaths.

"Napping?" Ranger Johnson's voice startled me. My eyes flew open. The sun was behind him, so I had to squint and tilt my head back to see him.

"No sir. Just . . . thinking," I said, when it seemed like he wanted more. The back of my neck prickled.

He squatted down and gestured at my book. "A journal?"

Before, I would have responded in a second, without thinking. But now? Now I was careful about what I revealed—even to adults. Words and choices could be used against you in ways you'd never dream, by people you'd never consider.

"Kind of." I waited.

So did he.

He tapped the cover of my notebook.

"There's lots to discover on these islands," he said. "If you know where to look." He paused. "You remember what we talked about yesterday?"

I met his gaze. He was smiling, but there was something funny about the area around his eyes—it was tight, like his eyes weren't smiling at all.

Knock it off, paranoid guy. You're imagining things.

I swallowed hard and smiled. "I do."

"Follow me," he said, and we walked into the woods, toward the fort. "Remember the story of Long Ben Avery?" he asked when we were far enough away for his liking.

I nodded.

"There's more. Avery was a pirate who pillaged ships all over the world. When pirates accumulated treasure, they'd hide parts of it in different ports, in case they were ever captured or needed to pay someone off—or disappear. We have documentation that shows that Long Ben hid treasure on Gallops Island almost three hundred years ago. It's never been found."

This was like the ultimate geocache.

"So who's looking for it?" I asked.

Ranger Johnson looked at me like I had nine heads. "Everyone," he said slowly.

"Everyone?" I repeated, skeptical. I mean, you didn't hear about it on the news or anything.

"Everyone who knows anything about treasure hunting," the ranger explained. I could tell he was trying to be patient—his voice was calm, but the tight lines around the side of his mouth revealed that he was struggling to keep it that way. "And we have to find it before someone else does. That treasure belongs in a museum."

Hadn't I heard that line in a movie somewhere?

"So the Parks Service is looking for the treasure?"

Ranger Johnson stepped back, like the question hurt him.

"This is unofficial business," he said. "Of course the Parks Service is looking for it, but it can't afford the man-hours to staff such a venture. That's where you come in."

Seriously? He expected me to buy this? I mean, I was no expert—but I did have some rather recent experience dealing with shady situations. And this definitely sounded shady.

"So you want me to help you find it. For the Parks Service," I added.

"Yes. For the Parks Service," he repeated. "You're good at finding stuff—that's obvious—and you have more . . . flexibility than I do in searching some of the sites on the island. I've done the research on where to look, all you have to do is go there and check out the sites."

Shady or not, there was no harm in looking. And if it had been hidden for three hundred years, the chances of me turning anything up would be small.

And seriously, it was *pirate treasure*. Who *doesn't* want to find pirate treasure on an island?!

"I don't need to tell you this is between us, and the other members of my team."

"Team?"

He eyed me. "Of course you're not the only one looking. And from what I understand, you work well with a partner anyway."

Did everyone think of me as a sidekick? I was going to get a complex.

"So there's Derek," he went on. Awesome. "And Grey."

Of course.

"She has her own boat. You never know where she'll turn up." He looked past me, into the trees. "Or when I will. So keep this on the down low."

He rubbed a hand—a big, work-outside park ranger hand—across my hat and tugged on the brim.

"Rest up," he said.

"Yes, sir," I said, but I wasn't sure he heard me over the thudding of my heart.

Here's how you get in major trouble on your summer vacation: Agree to search for pirate treasure.

DAY 5

CHRIS'S GOTCHA! ALIVE/TAGGED LIST

STEVE

D-BAG DEREK

~~ME (CHRIS)~~

JACK

MANNY

DOUG

PETE

~~HORATIO~~

CAM

~~JORGE~~

RAVI

OLLIE

10

Between Jack's early-morning wake-up, camp activities, and running into Grey and Ranger Johnson, I was exhausted—but sleep was hard to come by. So much swirled in my head.

Correction: A lot of stuff about Grey and the pirate treasure was swirling around my head.

Girls never bugged me like they bugged other guys, maybe because my best friend is a girl. In junior high, when kids coupled up, Moxie and I got teased for being together all the time—but we never liked each other like *that*. I swear, I even stopped thinking of her as a girl. She was just Moxie: math-obsessed, a little on the weird side, but very cool.

Grey was different—definitely different from Moxie, and different from the other girls in my grade. They were hair-flippy and giggly and couldn't look at most of the boys. Grey didn't seem that way at all. She was annoying. And rude. And frustrating . . . but interesting. And it was either think about her, or Long Ben Avery's treasure.

I had a million questions about that too, including one big one: What *was* the treasure, exactly? I mean, if it was paper money or something, it might be gone by now. Was it gold coins? Was that even a real thing, outside of the pirates of the whatever movie?

So it was a long time before I finally fell asleep.

Which is why it totally sucked to be woken up before dawn—*again*.

"Ollie! Ollie!" Chris nudged me and I snuggled the sweatshirt I'd rolled to use as a pillow. "C'mon! Get up! We'll miss the boat!"

Boat?

I opened one eye. The light inside of our tent was pale and weak.

"Whazzup?"

"The boat!" He kicked at the platform under my sleeping bag. "To Gallops. Come on!"

That boat. We'd been assigned to go to one of the islands to clean up storm damage. Even though it was closed to the public, Ranger Johnson got the okay from the Park Service for us to go. They said as long as we stayed outside, it was safe.

"I'm gonna skip it," I said, and turned back to my pillow.

"Okay." The disappointment in Chris's voice was so thick it nearly dripped onto the floor. "I'll tell Ranger Johnson you won't be coming to Gallops."

Gallops. Gallops . . . My muzzy brain finally made the connection. *Gallops!* That's where Long Ben Avery had hidden his treasure.

"Wait!" I called. Chris was already out of the tent, but he stuck his head back in, grinning.

"Give me two seconds." I scrambled out of my sleeping bag, grabbed my inhaler, and took my allergy pill. Manny and Jack were still lumps inside their sleeping bags, lucky guys. Digging through my laundry, I pulled out a T-shirt and tugged it on while I chewed on my toothpaste-smeared dry toothbrush.

"That's gross."

I shrugged.

I spat a wad of toothpaste outside the tent flap and followed Chris to the dock. The sky was barely pink.

Grey was on the boat. Well, she was helping to pack the boat, anyway.

She smiled at me and waved. Chris saw.

"What is she doing here? Why is she waving at you? Do you think she's coming with us, 'cause I think that's illegal—okay, not illegal, but against Wilderness Scout rules to have a non-troop member on an outing. Do we need to tell someone—"

"Chris! Dude!" I waved my hand in front of his face and he came out of his "talking-trance." "She's Ranger Johnson's *daughter*. I'm sure it's fine."

"Oh." That stopped him for a second or two. "Well, hey—maybe we'll see those porpoises again, huh? Wouldn't that be cool, to see them from the boat?" He went on.

Not a lot of kids were picked for the trip, evidently. Me and Chris were the only ones from our tent. Doug and Horatio were working on their community service to meet Discovery class requirement—Discovery is the last step before Master Scout—and . . .

"Awesome," whispered Chris. "Someone doesn't look pretty this early in the morning."

Derek. Deep scowl, bed-head; and "stay away from me" exuded from every pore.

"Awesome," I echoed. Then I realized: Ranger Johnson had set it up.

Ranger Johnson broke my train of thought. "Okay everyone, in the boat." Was he going to give us special instructions for looking for the treasure? Was there something I was supposed to do?

It was a small speedboat, with the National Parks Service logo painted on the sides. There were seats for eight people, and we were smooshed together. I was right next to Grey, my leg next to hers, with like a millimeter of space between us. I was afraid to relax, in case my leg crossed that imaginary barrier. I did *not* want Grey to think I liked her like that. At all. So I sat straight and stiff.

"Afraid of boats?" she asked, smiling that too-big smile at me.

"Uh, no," I said. "It's just . . . I just . . ." I couldn't tell her that I didn't want to touch her. That's crazy. Or creepy. Or both. The boat accelerated, and I scrabbled for something to hang on to so I wouldn't be thrown into Grey when it pulled out. I stretched my arm out behind me and grabbed on to a cleat—which was like putting my arm around her. Great.

Derek was across from me, legs stretched out in front of him, head lolling back on his shoulders; his posture was the exact opposite of mine. Grey leaned over and said something to him that I couldn't hear. They laughed.

The engine roared. The boat jounced over the waves, slamming me into the seat—and into Grey.

"Sorry!" I cried. I was sure my ears were pink. I scuttled away from her. My arm ached with the strain of holding my body still in the rocking, bouncing boat.

Across the aisle, Derek gave me a sly wink.

"Nice one, Doc!" he called.

Jerk.

We pulled up to Gallops. Derek, showing off his mad boating skills, jumped out and tied us to a cleat while Ranger Johnson slowly guided the boat parallel to the dock. As soon as I could, I put some space between Grey and me. Sweat trickled down my back.

"Let's go, boys," called Ranger Johnson. "Grey, can you get the bags?"

Grey headed into the compartment at the front of the boat, and I finally was able to breathe. I turned to the island.

It looked like Lovells: a stretch of beach, a hump of trees, not much else. There weren't any buildings on this one, just foundations and ruins.

One by one, we scrambled out of the boat and onto the small pier.

"Careful," cautioned the ranger. "As a reminder: This island is in more disrepair than the others. Due to the presence of asbestos, there hasn't been any development here. In fact, it's been closed for quite some time. You're here under special permission and need to stay away from the foundations."

Ranger Johnson wasn't kidding when he said "disrepair." The concrete walkways were cracked and broken, with chunks heaved up from the frost like waves on the harbor. We picked our way carefully from the pier across the beach, to one of the grassy hills. From there, we had a great view of the Boston skyline and a bunch of the other islands. Although it was clear on the harbor, a haze hung over the city. Another hot day.

The ranger told us about the storm damage: One of the retaining walls had cracked, and we needed to fortify it and clear some brush so the Parks Service could come in and mow the grass trails at that end of the island.

Derek muttered something about it being a waste of money to maintain trails on an island that people couldn't even visit.

"We should be looking for treasure, instead," Derek continued, dripping with sarcasm. "Now *that* would be a good use of our time!"

I couldn't help it, I gasped. Ranger Johnson had told us not to say anything—Derek was there. That meant Ranger Johnson hadn't told Derek anything specific, yet. Would he fill him in and somehow have us work together? Not cool.

"I'll make good use of your time," Ranger Johnson said to him. "You're with me. We can speculate all morning about where this so-called treasure is."

"Don't forget the rabbits." Grey was at her dad's elbow. "They're everywhere."

"There's an infestation on this island," he clarified. "They've actually destroyed a lot of vegetation, and the Parks Service is working with environmental groups to determine the best course of action for dealing with them. They're not very intimidated by humans, so they'll get close."

Chris and I were given the north end of the retaining wall, Horatio and Doug had another section. I wasn't sure where the ranger and Derek would be. Grey would go group to group with water and snacks.

We headed off, Chris pointing out the vegetation along the way—he wanted to earn a plant identification badge this week—and I finally relaxed once Grey was out of my sight.

"Here's our spot," I said. We were at the northwest corner of the island. Two rabbits nibbled at the sea grass on the edge of the wall. They looked at me curiously, heads cocked, like I was an intruder on their property. I guess I was. When I dropped my pack, they hopped away a few feet, then resumed munching.

The storm damage wasn't so bad out here. We spotted some holes in the wall that we were supposed to fill with loose rocks, and a few areas of brush that needed to be dragged off the path. Even though the rangers hadn't mowed out here in a few weeks, it was easy to see where the line of the path was—the grass wasn't as tall as the weeds around it.

"Wall first?" I asked. Chris nodded and we got to work.

It didn't take us long to finish the wall, but heaving rocks and broken pieces of granite in the sun had us sweating buckets. Chris even stopped talking, he was so hot. We plopped down, our backs to the wall, to take a break. Like magic, Grey appeared with two icy bottles of water.

"Looks good," she said, "for a couple of amateurs." Couldn't she just be nice?

Chris protested, then launched into a description of what

we'd done. I tuned him out and watched Grey. Although she'd been in the sun and trekking around the island, she seemed unbothered by the heat. Her hair was pulled back at the base of her neck, and a stray strand blew in the hot breeze.

"We're gonna clear the tree limbs from the path next," Chris continued, "and I hope there's no poison ivy there. Pete is miserable with it. I'm getting my plant identification badge this week and I've been watching for it, but I haven't seen any yet—at least, I don't think I've seen it. I might have and just not known it."

Grey looked at me with raised eyebrows: An "Is this kid for real?" look. I grinned.

"Want to see something cool?" she said, interrupting Chris. She wore a devilish expression on her face. "You can't tell my dad, though. He gets all freaked out when I explore parts of the island without his permission, and he's extra stressed because my mom's in Milwaukee for some conference this week."

Immediately, we both nodded. She led us away from the path, toward a rocky bulge in the grass. It was the foundation for one of the old buildings. My stomach tightened.

"We're not supposed to be near this stuff," Chris said.

Grey stopped. "Okay. I can take you guys back. Maybe Derek or the other guys would be interested? It's pretty cool."

I elbowed Chris. No way was I losing out to Derek. "We're in."

She stayed still for another minute, considering. "C'mon." She passed the foundation, and my stomach loosened a little. She scrambled down a hill past the ruined building. "Don't fall in," she called over her shoulder.

We followed. The gravelly sand and soft beach grass made

it hard for my feet to catch any traction, and I skated down the hill.

Instead of ending at a beach, as I expected, we were at a funny spot on the island: the intersection of the retaining wall that wrapped the north side of the island, and the beach. And right in front of us, covered in plants and nearly hidden from view, was a cave.

Grey was halfway inside.

11

Here's how you get in trouble when you find a cave:

Follow people into it.

"Ollie, where are you?" Grey's voice reached over the whoosh of the waves beyond a sand berm that had washed into the mouth of the cave. Chris raced to follow her, his sneakers disappearing between thick sea grass and vines.

I climbed the hill of sand, dropped to my belly, and slid through the curtain of green. Was this another example of my "sidekick syndrome"—just following without thinking? But I pushed the thought away. This was a *real cave*! Who cared who found it?

My eyes, used to the bright sun from the beach, couldn't process the change and I couldn't see *anything*—just blackness. Head first, I slid down the sand berm, into the cave—and into Chris's sneakers. The sound of the surf echoed through the chamber. For a dizzying minute I couldn't tell which way was up. Panicked, I tried to sit, flailing my arms and legs and reaching for something to orient me.

I hit someone, instead. Someone soft.

Grey grunted. "Easy there, Ollie!" A click, and then a flashlight beam pierced the darkness. My breathing slowed. I sat up like a normal person, brushing the sand off my T-shirt.

Grey swept the beam around. Chris was to my left, back to a wall. The cave was small, with rock walls, and, except for us, some sand, and the noise of the waves, was completely empty.

"How'd you find this place?" Chris asked. His voice echoed in the room, just like the surf. It must've surprised him, because he stopped with just one question.

"I've been all over these islands." Grey spoke from behind the flashlight, like the great and powerful Oz. "I know all the good hiding places."

What was she hiding? Or hiding from?

"Ever find anything in them?" It was a late jab, and kind of low, but she'd earned it for all her snarky comments to me.

"None of your business," she snapped.

"So, let's see what's going on in here," Chris said, trying for distraction. It worked.

Grey swung the flashlight around again. "There isn't much more to it," she said. "It doesn't go anywhere, except . . ." She pointed the flashlight at what would be the back corner (even though the cave was kind of bowl shaped). At first, I couldn't see what the big deal was—it was just dirt. Then, as I looked more closely . . .

"Is that *writing?*" Chris breathed.

It was. Scratched into the cave wall were what appeared to be letters. We crowded closer: Cpt. A 16—. The other numbers were too faded to read.

"It's initials or something," Grey said. "I'm pretty sure they're

Long Ben Avery's. He was a pirate who stashed part of his treasure here."

"Seriously?" I played skeptic, trying to figure out what Grey was doing and hide the thrumming in my chest. Had I already found the treasure Ranger Johnson was looking for? Was that even possible? "I thought the pirate treasure was gone."

"Duh. That was *Captain Kidd. His* treasure is gone." She turned the flashlight beam on herself, frowning. "I have lived out here, like, *my whole life.* I know all the stories about this place. No one knows where this cave is—not even my dad. He's a big pirate buff too. Especially when it comes to Long Ben Avery. Gotta know all the stories about treasure to tell the tourists." She rolled her eyes.

I pressed. "Then why haven't you told him about this place?"

"Because he's super-intense about what I'm allowed to do," Grey said. "He'd probably take away my boat if he knew I was here. He'd say it wasn't safe."

My eyes had adjusted to the dimness of the light coming in through the top of the cave's opening. Chris's head swiveled back and forth as he followed our argument.

"So what's so great about Long Ben Avery?" Chris asked.

"Here, sit," Grey said. We sat in a circle, legs crossed like story time at the library.

"Long Ben was only one of the most successful pirates in history," Grey went on, after she propped the flashlight at her knees. "He robbed an Indian treasure ship, with hundreds of thousands of pounds of jewels, and got away with it. He paid off his men, and his whole crew retired. He changed his name and was never heard from again. Supposedly he died in Ireland."

"If he died in Ireland, what was he doing here?" Chris was just getting warmed up. "And Indians didn't have treasure— they had, like, canoes and corn and stuff. And you're not even supposed to call them that, anyway. They're Native Americans."

Grey pointed the flashlight right in Chris's eyes. He stopped talking.

"I *know* they're Native Americans," she said, exasperated. "I'm talking about *India* Indians! Long Ben got into a fight with the ship and took it over. He couldn't go anywhere the British owned, so he sailed toward North America with his loot. Rumor is he stopped in the Bahamas, then came up the East Coast, then crossed to Ireland from Boston. He stashed little bits of treasure in different places in case he got caught and needed to buy his way out of trouble, just like Captain Kidd."

"That doesn't prove that he wrote this," I pointed out. "Any- one could have. It could be thirty years old, not three hundred."

"First of all, no one could have written this thirty years ago, because up until five years ago this stretch of beach was part of the hill, expert. They removed part of the hill in the 1800s, and there was an avalanche when they did that. When they extended the sea wall a few years ago, they excavated some of the land that collapsed. I found it last summer." I couldn't totally tell, but I think she folded her arms after that.

"Sorry, but I'm with Grey on this one, Ollie," said Chris. "This is real pirate writing. Why'd he write it? Did he hide something in here? Is it the treasure? Or maybe he killed some- one and buried them here?"

"There's nothing here," said Grey. "I've checked a bunch of times. I just thought this was a cool place to show you." Her tone was as icy as it was hot outside. We stood.

Should've kept your mouth shut, Ollie, I thought. I stepped to the wall, then reached out to touch the words. They were carved deeper into the rock than they looked. Years of salt had accumulated in the letters and made them white, like they'd been scratched with chalk. Grey was right. Long Ben Avery had made his mark here.

I turned around to apologize, and I must not have been as adjusted to the dark as I thought I was, because I lost the sense of up and down again. The dizziness came back and I pitched forward. I stuck out an arm to prevent myself from falling, only instead of grabbing rock wall, my arm pushed through it. There was a loud, brittle *crack!* and pain shot across my wrist. For a second, I thought the noise was my arm breaking. I tipped sideways, following my arm.

"Ohmygod!" It came out of Grey like one word. "Ollie!"

And Chris, at the same time: "Ollie, you okay?! Are you hurt? I know first aid!"

My lungs disappeared; the shock of the fall triggered an asthma attack. I couldn't get air. I grabbed for my inhaler with my free hand and took a deep puff.

"Fine," I wheezed. "'M okay." I huffed again.

Grey directed the flashlight at the source of the noise: My arm had pushed right through the cave wall, and was stuck just above the elbow.

"Can you move it?" Grey held the flashlight between her chin and shoulder, the way my mom holds the phone when she's making dinner and talking to Aunt Cathy.

"Yeah." I wiggled my fingers, expecting the searing, burning pain of a broken bone—like when I'd busted my ankle in fourth grade and it hurt to move my toes. Surprisingly, nothing felt like that. "I think I'm cool. The cracking noise wasn't from me." What *did* hurt, though, were the million scratches and prickles up and down my arm. The cave didn't have a rock wall after all—it was made of wood.

In the hole, my fingers bumped against some cold rocks. And something soft and crumbly. A shudder ran through me. What was in there? Bones? Something . . . else? What if something bit me? I jerked my arm. Shooting pain from the scratches. I hissed against it.

"Careful, Ollie! Don't move it!" That was Chris.

"Easy for you to say. This is creeping me out."

"Can you feel anything in there?" Grey asked hopefully.

I had to get a grip—ha-ha. I took a breath, let it out slowly. Coughed. Then I stretched out my fingers: same soft, crumbly stuff, and rocks. This was the worst game of "what's in the bag" ever.

"There's something soft and crumbly, like old paper. And some rocks." *Please don't let anything bite me. Please don't let anything bite me . . .*

"Oh! Maybe it's money!" Grey's eyes flashed in the dim light.

"Or jewels!" That was Chris.

83

"Guys, let's get my arm out and we can actually *see* what's in here." Had I found the treasure? If so, what next? Should we tell the ranger?

Grey and Chris broke a few pieces of wood from around my arm, so I could pull it out without getting a second set of scratches. I was grateful that Mom had made me get that tetanus shot before I left for camp, even though I wasn't sure you could get tetanus from wood.

I jerked my arm from the hole, and blood slid toward my wrist. Grey used the flashlight.

My right forearm looked like it had been attacked by Pinocchio's feral cat: scratches from my fingers to bicep, a few gouges, and splinters galore. For a second, I flashed back to Moxie throwing herself down the last couple of steps at the T station to manufacture an injury so her mom wouldn't find out where we'd actually been that night. Moxie'd be impressed with this.

Then the throbbing started.

"Doesn't look like it's going to fall off," Chris said helpfully. "But you should definitely get those splinters out and get it checked out by Mr. Fuentes and Ranger Johnson. What are we going to say happened to you?"

"We aren't going to be able to do or say anything until we get out of here," I pointed out. "It might not be that bad in daylight." I was lying. It'd probably look worse.

It was obvious that I'd live. Grey swung the flashlight to the hole.

"Look," she breathed.

The beam didn't provide a ton of light, but it was easy to see what had happened: The cave "wall" was really brittle wood. Filthy from age and weather, it had camouflaged itself to the surrounding rock. There was no way to tell the difference from just looking at it.

Following the beam of light, Chris and I peered into the jagged hole.

"Holy shnikey!" he cried.

Holy shnikey. The space was a cubby about as large as one of the boxes of copy machine paper that my dad brings home from his office for LeeLee to decorate and turn into ships or rockets or cars.

The bottom was filled with rocks and tatters of material. Gingerly, Grey reached in and pulled a piece out.

"Maybe it was some kind of bag?" Chris guessed when Grey held the strip up. It felt more like tissue paper than cloth. Years of sitting in the cave had destroyed it.

"What was in it?" Grey wondered.

I shrugged. "Money, maybe? If so, it's long gone. The paper would have disintegrated." I hope-hope-hoped that neither of them decided to grab one of those rocks to investigate. Because I was starting to think that those "rocks" weren't rocks at all. And even though Grey called us a "team," I wasn't sure we were playing the same game.

Besides, one thing I'd learned this summer was that when it comes to items that have been missing for a while, finding them can be really, really complicated.

We had to get out of the cave. I had to get them out of the cave.

"Uh . . . guys? My arm?" I'd been holding it across my body

85

while they investigated the faulty cave wall, but it was seriously throbbing and regardless of what was in Long Ben Avery's hidey-hole, I needed medical attention.

"Let's go," Grey said. She took another look at the hole and headed to the exit.

I took out my portable GPS and flipped it on.

"What're you doing?" Chris asked. Grey was halfway up the sand berm and squirming out the exit.

"Marking the cache," I replied. "Habit." I needed to be able to find this cave again. Soon.

Chris went up the berm next, and I followed. My arm was killing me: The skin felt tight with swelling.

When we got back outside, I was surprised that it was still daytime—like going to a matinee movie and coming out into the parking lot, it felt like a whole day had passed. According to the sun, we'd been in the cave for less than an hour.

And the sun revealed the full extent of the damage I'd done: Red scratches spiderwebbed my forearm, and around the splinters the skin looked puffy and inflamed already. A long, thin cut traveled from the inside of my wrist and wound to my elbow. Blood oozed and dripped all over my shorts and T-shirt. The sight made me woozy.

"Oh, Ollie," Grey said. At that second, I didn't care that I didn't trust her, or was keeping a secret from Chris. I just wanted to lie down.

"Dude," Chris breathed. "That is gnarly."

I pinched a splinter of wood the size of a toothpick between two fingers and pulled it out. It stung. Blood welled in the spot. The pain took my mind off my thudding heart and anxiety.

"We can't tell my dad where we were," Grey said. "He doesn't know about the cave, and I'm not supposed to bring you guys around on this island. It's dangerous."

"Duh," Chris said. "But what about the piece of fabric? From the bag? I mean, what if it held treasure or something—"

"We say nothing," Grey interrupted. "*Nothing.* Get it? There was nothing in there."

"So what are we supposed to say about *this?*" I gestured to my mangled arm with my whole one.

"You can say that you fell down the retaining wall," Chris said, "and landed in some branches." He pointed to a spot near where we'd been working, where a tangle of driftwood rested against the base of the wall. "Like over there."

I removed another splinter or two. More blood.

"He's not going to buy it."

"He will." Grey nodded her head rapidly. "He totally will. I'll say that when I found you and Chris when I came to get you water, you were horsing around and fell. Happens all the time."

"You'll look like an idiot," Chris said cheerfully, "but the location of the cave will be safe."

"Everyone promise," Grey said. "No one says anything about the cave."

The two of them exchanged grins. Anxiety prickled my neck. I didn't trust Grey, but I didn't want to tell anyone about the cave either.

"Fine." I said. "Promise." Chris promised too.

I surveyed my bloody arm. "Chris, let's bust out your first aid skills."

"Yeah, team!" Grey cheered as Chris started plucking the biggest splinters.

Yeah, right.

DAY 6

CHRIS'S GOTCHA! ALIVE/TAGGED LIST

STEVE

D-BAG DEREK

~~ME (CHRIS)~~

JACK

MANNY

DOUG

PETE

~~HORATIO~~

CAM

~~JORGE~~

RAVI

OLLIE

12

Ranger Johnson gave me a skeptical look when he saw my arm and heard our "horsing around" story, but I'm guessing he thought Chris and I were doing something stupider than we admitted to. I couldn't tell him what I thought I found, but I had to get back to Gallops to do more searching. Grey's "team" declaration made me feel more like "every man for himself."

Back on Lovells, Scoutmaster Fuentes turned my scratched-up arm into a troop-wide first aid lesson. *That* stunk. I had to suffer through two kids wrapping me in bandages and applying almost an entire tube of antibiotic ointment after I was de-splintered. Jack's eyes nearly fell out of his head when he saw me.

Dr. Gupta kept asking me if I needed to go home, which freaked out Mr. F. They were worried that I was going to sue or something.

But I couldn't go home even if I wanted to (which I didn't). I needed to wait 'til the media moved on to something else . . . a park ranger, his daughter, and a Wilderness Scout finding long-lost pirate treasure, for instance. And that scout could be Chris, not me. I could happily be in the background and let them take the spotlight *away* from me.

The more I thought about it, the better the idea seemed. The media would be so excited about *their* find that the business Moxie and I were involved in with the Gardner art would just drift away. I just had to actually find the treasure. And the rocks in the cave were as good a place as any to start.

At least Chris and Grey didn't investigate the hole too carefully. But what if Grey went back, alone? She did have her own boat. If she found them, and my name got attached to the story, the media insanity would be nothing compared to what my family had already been through. Something else to worry about.

Needless to say, with a bandaged, throbbing arm, and a head full of what I may have found, I barely slept. Manny snuck out for his midnight swim, and I counted the minutes until he came back. I couldn't get comfortable. And Chris snored.

Were those rocks actually jewels? Were they really part of Long Ben Avery's Indian treasure? As much as I wanted to stay out of the spotlight, I still wanted to know the truth.

The top of the tent lightened. I rubbed my eyes—they were gritty, like they'd been sprinkled with beach sand—and gave up on sleep for the night. Slipping out of my sleeping bag, I tugged on blood-free, cleanish clothes, and went to the remains of the campfire to tend to my wounded arm. A few rabbits hopped by the logs we used for seating. They didn't seem to mind my company.

The bandages were bloody and slick with ointment. I dabbed ointment from the first aid bag on the deepest punctures and across the giant scratch, and did my best to wind the clean bandages around my arm.

I balanced my notebook on my knee. Although it was awkward, I could still write and sketch despite the mess of my arm. Absently, I drew the entrance to the cave, then shaded the water around it.

Typically when I log a cache, I draw the site and jot down the GPS coordinates. But something didn't feel right about that, so I left the coordinates off the image. Instead, I paged back to a cache I'd logged on the Boston Common earlier in the summer, and jotted the coordinates there, so I could clear them from my GPS. I'd be able to find the cave, no problem, no matter how much time passed before I went there again.

After I finished, I wasn't sure what to do next. I tapped my pencil on the notebook's cover and stared at the sky. And then a hand clapped over my mouth, and I screamed.

I also slid backward off the log, into whoever grabbed me. I didn't even think: Just kicked the log, pushing as hard as I could to drive the person behind me into the ground, and threw my bandaged elbow into them like Agent Goh had told me. I had to get away, fast.

"Oof! Ollie! Knock it off!" The hand slipped from my mouth, and hands shoved my shoulders.

Chris.

I rolled onto my side so he could crawl out from under me.

"You nearly killed me!"

"You snuck up on me!"

We were nose to nose. I was breathing hard, heart pounding. Chris's eyes were wide and he rubbed his ribs.

"What the heck?!" he said. "What's that about? Can't you take a joke?"

For a second, I almost told him: No, I can't take a joke. Not anymore. Because even though you think what I did this summer was amazing, bad guys had chased me—for real. And it was terrifying. But I bit the words back.

Ashamed, I dropped my eyes to the ground. Sand and scorched wood dotted the grass.

"Sorry," I told him. "I didn't expect anyone else to be up this early."

"Yeah, well, we probably woke the whole camp," Chris said. He scowled, but didn't appear as angry as he had a second ago. "With moves like that, you'll win Gotcha! for sure. You're like Charlie Jihn, that action hero. Are you a trained ninja? 'Cause that would be so cool."

Despite how bad I felt, I cracked a smile.

"So what were you doing out here, anyway?"

"Couldn't sleep." We rolled the log that I'd knocked out of place back to where it belonged and sat down. Chris picked up one of the long sticks we used to prod the fire, and drew designs in the sand around the pit.

"Do you think there may have been treasure in that cave? Like, at one point?"

He looked so hopeful, like his whole world could change in an instant if the statement was true. And honestly, it would.

"Probably," I said, and brought my gaze to the top of a log. "Looks that way."

"I can't believe you're not more excited about this," Chris said. "It's amazing. We found an old pirate hiding spot! We're going to be *famous!*"

I couldn't help it, I cringed. "Trust me, you don't want that attention," I said.

"Easy for you to say," he said. "You're already famous. You *have* money. I'm going to Chestnut College Prep this fall on scholarship, and my parents are totally stressed over the stuff that the scholarship money *doesn't* cover. If we found something real, it could make things so much better."

My brain ran in a bunch of different directions: One—Ranger Johnson told me not to tell anyone that I was supposed to be looking for the treasure. Two—I didn't want the newspapers to know I found it—even though, to be honest, I kind of *wanted* to find it (it was *pirate treasure* after all!). Three—I hadn't really found anything—I just *thought* I did. What I saw—and felt—in the cave could just be, well, rocks. And four—I trusted Chris. He was a good guy; I knew that. We were on the same team.

I took a deep breath.

"Can you keep a secret?"

"What the heck, Ollie?! Who are you, Indiana Jones Junior?"

I finished telling Chris about the treasure and how Ranger Johnson had Derek and me looking for it. He cracked up at the craziness of the situation.

"What a dream team," he said, laughing. "Oh man."

"Yeah," I muttered, a wave of exhaustion rolling over me. "More like the Nightmare Squad."

"Well," he added, "you have Grey. And me."

"I'm not sure she makes me feel any better," I said. "Something's not right there."

The rest of the camp started to wake up, so we stopped talking about it.

To relax, I decided to do some straight up orienteering and caching. Mr. Fuentes ordered me to stick to light activities until my scratches were scabbed over—a disgusting infection would not be a good way to end the summer—so I asked him if I could set up some caches for the other scouts, instead of working on a wilderness badge. He agreed, as long as I brought a buddy.

I stuffed my pack with snacks, water, some origami paper, a sandwich bag of plastic toy cars—the cheapie ones little kids find in goody bags at birthday parties—and extra batteries for my GPS. Chris and Manny were working on advanced lifesaving at the docks, but Jack, who'd finished plant identification, said he'd join me. I stressed out for a minute, hoping that Chris would keep our secret, but Mr. F. didn't want me near the salt water, so it's not like I could join them. I just hoped Chris didn't let his mouth get ahead of his brain.

"What're the toys and paper for?" Jack asked. He wasn't big into caching.

"You'll see. Have you been down to the beach?" I said, changing the subject.

He shook his head. "Not since the morning we watched the porpoises. I seriously do not want a sunburn."

"Guess we'll stick to the inner island and fort, then."

Jack lathered himself with my SPF 30 sunscreen and pulled his hat down low. We headed out.

Following the trail to the fort was easy; we'd done it a million times. Once there, I slowed down and we did a loop around the perimeter. The walls were crumbling concrete, with tons of little holes in them. At the northeast corner, I stopped and squatted down.

"What're you doing?" Jack said. "This is why I don't do this stuff. It's lame."

"It's not lame," I responded. "You just haven't done one right yet." I slid my backpack off and fished through it for a sheet of origami paper. Quickly, I folded it into a small box.

"How'd you learn to do that? Did your mom or dad teach you?"

I shook my head. Why do so many kids think all Asian people are the same? "I'm part Vietnamese, not Japanese," I explained. "My mom is white, and my parents don't know how to do origami. I watched a video online. It's easy. Look." I showed him as I made the final crease, and held up my finished box. Then I took one of the toy cars out of my pack and slipped it inside. With a pen, I numbered the cache and drew my Oxenfree icon on the bottom. This was the 200th cache I'd hidden.

"Now we hide it." As I spoke, I had the funny feeling that we were being watched. I scanned the trees around the fort, but there were so many leaves and bushes they were impossible to see through.

The paper I'd chosen was a flat gray, similar in shade to

the walls of the bunker. Jack's eyes brightened. He was starting to get it.

"Here," he said. A fist-sized chunk of wall had crumbled at knee level, leaving an indentation small enough for the box. I checked the trees again. I couldn't shake the sensation. We stuck the cache in the hole, then put a few small pieces of concrete on top. When we stood, we couldn't see it unless we were really looking for it.

"There," I said. I checked my GPS for the coordinates, and put them in my notebook. "This'll be the starting point. From here, let's hide three more." I handed my GPS to Jack and showed him how it worked.

Something blurred by the corner of my eye, and I moved my head just in time to see someone dart behind a tree. Another scout.

"Act natural," I whispered to Jack from the side of my mouth. "Someone's in the trees. It's Gotcha! time." We each assumed we were the target.

"Run to the opposite trees, on three," Jack said. "I'm gonna climb. You?"

There weren't many people I could outrun, and my stubby legs and scratched arm weren't going to help me get airborne. "I'll hide," I said.

"One, two . . ." Before Jack got to three, the kid raced out from behind his tree. The kamikaze approach.

"Run!" Jack shouted. The scout had about two dozen yards to cover. We raced for the trees.

Heart slamming, I ran as fast as I could and didn't look back.

Sneakers pounded the ground. Ahead of me, a rabbit bolted.

Jack was a body length ahead of me. Our pursuer picked up the pace. Jack cleared the sun/tree line and jumped for a low-hanging branch.

He missed.

The other scout passed me and, trying to tackle Jack, also leaped. But Jack was already on the ground, so the bigger kid found himself flying at nothing—except a tree trunk. He slammed into it with his shoulder and went down with a howl.

Jack took advantage and sprang to his feet. He climbed the tree like LeeLee's favorite monkey, Curious George, and hung on to a branch. I stopped next to the kid.

"You okay?"

It was Steve. He nodded and rubbed his shoulder under his Hellcats marching band T-shirt.

"Wind knocked out of me." He looked up at Jack. "You've gotta come down sometime, Red. Then you're mine."

Jack went up another branch or two, then settled in, back against the trunk. "Pass me my pack, Ols?"

Steve scowled at me. See, the thing about chasing someone into a tree is that while you're climbing up, the person you're after can just drop down and get a head start on you. On the other hand, everyone has to come down sometime. And both Jack and Steve would have to appear at lunch, or the Gotcha! game would be blown. They had two hours.

I went back to the base of the fort and grabbed Jack's bag. When I handed it up to him—around the far side of the tree from where Steve was standing—I shrugged at Steve. Jack was my tent-mate. No way was I going to give Steve the advantage.

Steve sat at the base of the tree and took a book out of his pocket. Although setting up the other caches wasn't appealing, I knew I had to for the same reason that Jack would eventually have to come out of the tree—we'd get caught if I didn't.

I walked deeper into the trees, marked two spots, quickly folded boxes and dropped a toy car in each. I hid them, marked the coordinates, then went back to Jack's tree.

"You knock anyone out yet?" Steve asked. I shook my head. Pete's poison ivy . . . well . . . let's just say it had spread. Miserable, he'd been hanging out by the tents and campfire until his condition lightened up. I still had no idea who had me, though. Six days in and no attempt? The theory in our tent was that Pete also had me—a "draw," the guys called it. Usually that didn't happen until the end, but sometimes it worked out that way.

Jack shook the leaves. I glanced at him.

He mouthed: *I have to pee.*

I looked around. As far as I could tell, Jack had three options:

1. Hold it and stay in the tree until lunch.

2. Climb out of the tree and risk getting caught by Steve.

3. Stay in the tree and, well, solve his problem.

I raised my hands, palms up, like, "What do you want me to do?"

After a few seconds, Jack came to the same conclusions as I had. And by the expression on his face—which had broken into a devilish grin similar to Grey's—I knew which option he chose.

I gave Jack some privacy, expecting him to, er, water the grass.

With the thick cover of leaves on the trees, Jack was pretty much out of sight from the ground. The unmistakable jingle of a loosened belt buckle, then a zipper, came from the canopy. Steve, back to the trunk, tilted his head at the sound.

And then a stream of liquid fell from above—right onto Steve's head.

At first, I don't think he put it together. He sat, frozen, as it steadily dripped and splashed the pages of his book. Then, everything clicked. Shouting words that my mom would ground me for—and she could probably hear all the way in Jamaica Plain—he sprang off the grass like it was electrified. His book hit the dirt, and his feet pounded as he raced through the trees toward the beach.

Screams of "I am going to kill you, you little—" trailed from him.

Jack's feet appeared through the leaves, and he dropped the last four feet or so. By the time his sneakers were on land, I was doubled over, laughing hysterically at his prank. So was he. Tears dripped from his eyes.

"Did you see him?" I gasped. "Dude, you are so dead. Like, really dead."

Jack nodded, still howling. "I *know*! I don't care!" He was laughing so hard, he could barely breathe. "His face . . . oh my god, his *face*!"

I wiped tears from my own eyes. "You are *nasty*, dude. I can't believe you did that!"

My words made Jack laugh harder. Then, abruptly, he stopped laughing, stuck a hand in his backpack, and tossed something at me.

Instinctively, I caught. While I did, Jack took off, deeper into the trees.

It was his water bottle—empty.

The jingle of belt and zipper came from the woods.

DAY 7

CHRIS'S GOTCHA! ALIVE/TAGGED LIST

STEVE

D-BAG DEREK

~~ME (CHRIS)~~

JACK

MANNY

DOUG

PETE

~~HORATIO~~

CAM

~~JORGE~~

RAVI

OLLIE

13

"C'mon, man, *really*? Did Jack really pee on him?" Doug was the fifth guy to ask me over breakfast.

"Um," I said, mouth full of cereal. "That's gross. Seriously? Who would do that?"

Doug grinned. "I knew it!" he said. "Best prank *ever*. This is going down in troop history."

As he walked back to his tent, laughing, I caught Steve and Derek glowering at me. I turned away from them to wipe down my cereal bowl, and Mr. Fuentes was watching me too. I was getting paranoid.

Mr. Fuentes and Dr. Gupta knew something was going on with Jack—everyone had started calling Jack "Whiz," for one thing, and it wasn't in reference to the Wizard of Oz—but they chalked it up to summer camp shenanigans, and didn't ask.

Chris and Manny were bummed that they missed the whole thing. Chris was quiet for ten whole minutes as we told them the story (Jack and I kept cracking up in the middle, so it took a while to get out), then he spent the next forty minutes quizzing us on every detail.

Manny shook his head after our third or fourth retelling.

"You guys are crazy-dead. Derek is just adding stuff to the list you're on," he pointed out to me.

"It was worth it just to see the look on Steve's face," Jack said. "Seriously."

It was also worth it to give Chris something else to talk about.

Later that morning, I spotted Derek sitting with Steve, their backs to the rest of the group, whispering.

Plotting, most likely.

"Let's go for a walk," I said to Chris. We checked in with Mr. Fuentes, and told him we were going to do some work on plant identification. He waved us off, and we headed to the fort.

"Have you heard from Grey?" he asked. "'Cause maybe she can get us back to Gallops. Don't you want to go?"

I stopped him. "Yeah. Haven't seen her, though. I don't know that she's the best person to take us either."

We leaned against the wall.

"She's not the best person to take you where?" The deep voice came from the fort, behind us. Chris and I jumped a mile.

Ranger Johnson came out of the fort. He had bags under his eyes and looked a little tired.

"Um . . . nowhere," I said. I gulped, my ears as pink as they get.

Chris stared at the ground, silent. Ranger Johnson studied the two of us.

"Spill it," he said. I didn't look at Chris, but felt him shift beside me.

"You told him," he said to me, finally. I bit the inside of my cheek and nodded.

"Yes, sir." I braced myself for a wave of trouble.

Instead he rubbed his face and gave us a weak grin. "Okay. The more hands and eyes, the better."

Chris's floodgates opened. "Are you sure there's real pirate treasure there? I mean, it's been a long, long time and who knows what happened to it—we're pretty sure if it's money, it's gone, but there could be other stuff, like jewels, that aren't gone. Yet. But how do we get back there? And where do we look?"

Ranger Johnson jumped in while Chris took a breath. "Yes, I'm sure it's real. Yes, I'm sure it's there. I'm going to take you." He answered each one of Chris's questions, ticking them off on his fingers as he did so.

He turned to me, friendly and smiling. "Derek and I weren't very fruitful in our search the other day. Would you be willing to give it a go?"

"Of course," I responded. "We'd be happy to." Slowly, carefully, I stretched my leg out and stepped on Chris's foot. I did *not* want him telling the ranger that we had something specific to check out. Luckily, he seemed to get the message—or was in so much pain that he couldn't complain.

"Good. Be at the dock this afternoon, before dinner. I'll come up with something to tell Mr. Fuentes. And, Ollie—" He cut himself off and gave me a dark look. "When I say don't tell anyone, I mean *don't tell anyone*." Then he went back into the trees. With the constantly shifting light, it was hard to spot him.

"That was so weird! And so cool!" Chris held a high five for me to slap. As I did so, anxiety flooded me. There was something not quite right here. Not right at all.

But I couldn't think about it for another second, because two guys burst into the clearing: Doug, followed by Cam. Doug, sprinting at full speed, trying to make it back to camp. Cam powered behind him, barely an arm's length away.

We pressed against the fort as Doug blew by. Cam, face red and puffing, stretched, jumped. The two guys crashed at the base of a tree.

"Gotcha!" Cam yelled, stickering his shoulder.

Doug spat some sand out and brushed himself off. "Enjoy the show?" he grumbled at us.

We stayed quiet while he fished through his pockets and handed his stickers and target to Cam, who was puffing almost as much as I do when I need my inhaler.

The whistle signaling the end of morning sessions sounded, and the guys limped off.

"Remember," I said to Chris, "we have to keep this quiet. Don't tell anyone what's up, not even Manny or Jack. Promise?"

"Promise." We got ready to head back to camp.

"See you at the dock!" Grey's voice came from the fort as we were leaving the clearing. She'd been listening the whole time.

Trouble.

14

Chris, Manny, Jack, and I waited our turn for a water safety badge check on the dock. Cam, Jorge, and Ravi's tent group jumped in, and I cringed as the cool water splashed us. Even though it was totally irrational, I worried that I'd be dashed to death on the pilings that supported the pier.

Water stuff isn't my strong suit. My mom made me take swimming lessons as a little kid, but I'm not coordinated. I flail around in the water and my asthma kicks in pretty quick. In the Y pool, where I've done all of my water merit badge requirements, I get by okay. But swimming in Boston Harbor? With waves? And sea creatures? Or—more likely—weird trash from boats? That freaked me out.

My stomach twisted and chest tightened.

Wasn't there something about waiting for two hours after you ate before swimming anyway?

I backed away from our group to get my breathing under control. My bathing suit didn't have pockets, and I didn't want to be a wuss, so I hadn't brought my inhaler.

I closed my eyes and concentrated: In. Hold. Out. In. Hold. Out. After a few breaths, I felt less panicky and my chest relaxed. Chris nudged me, and I opened my eyes.

"We're next." Swim one hundred yards, tread water for two minutes, sail a boat—my personal triathlon of water hell.

I took one more breath. The planks on the dock were warm, but rough and splintery under my feet. Mr. Fuentes had a clipboard, and Poison Ivy Pete—my Gotcha! target—awkwardly held a stopwatch with bandaged hands. Beside me, the guys were ready: Jack reluctantly peeled off a long-sleeve shirt and kept an eye on the sun. Manny handed his glasses to Doug. Chris bounced on the balls of his feet, removing layer after layer.

"Can I do a cannonball, Mr. F.? I'll go first, so it won't be a hazard, but I really want to cannonball off the dock, and we're usually not allowed to jump off until the last day."

Mr. Fuentes didn't look up from his clipboard.

"Nope," he responded.

Chris's shoulders slumped. The dark water lapped at the underside of the dock. Tendrils of ropy sea gunk waved around the pilings.

Luckily, the water was calm today. Behind us, a couple of the guys were fooling around. I kept my eyes on the water, mesmerized, as their shouts and jeers bounced off its surface.

"And . . . *go*," said Mr. F.

I was in the middle of a last inhale when someone's shoulder slammed into the middle of my back, pushing me forward and off the dock. Panicked, I pinwheeled my arms, and my body hit the water starfish-style, instead of in a straight line. At least I kept my mouth shut.

The surprise at being shoved and the awkwardness of the fall sent a jolt of adrenaline through my body that competed with the shock of the cool water. The salt stung the scratches on my arm.

The prickling pain brought me back to myself and I kicked to the surface. I was fairly close to the pilings, and I pushed away, toward the open water.

Mr. Fuentes, Pete, and Derek—of course Derek—peered over the edge at me.

"You all right, Ollie?" Mr. Fuentes looked concerned.

"Yeah," I spluttered, nodding. It took all of my concentration to tread water and keep upright as the waves bobbed past my face.

"Sorry, dude. We were messing around and I lost my balance. Hope you're not hurt." Derek's apology was about as sincere as a grizzly apologizing to a salmon.

"'M fine," I muttered.

"You can begin treading water," Pete offered helpfully.

"I *am* treading water," I pointed out. "Doesn't this count?"

Mr. Fuentes nodded. "Give him thirty more seconds," he directed. At least this was good for something. "Derek will be sitting out the test as a consequence for not displaying proper safety measures near the water."

I waved my arms and treaded, getting myself together. The shove was payback for my role in the Steve/Jack prank. But Derek was walking a tight line. You don't mess with people around the ocean.

"Okay, you can begin your swim." I glanced around. Chris, Manny, and Jack were on the other side. We were supposed to head to a marker that was fifty yards away, then swim back.

Because of where I'd fallen in, I'd have to add another ten yards onto my swim. Awesome.

I kicked and paddled. When I finally finished, Mr. Fuentes told us that we'd passed part one and to get a boat.

Chris and I paired up for the boating test.

"I get seasick," Manny said. "Sitting this one out." Jack scurried across the sand for a patch of shade.

"Do you know how to do this?" Chris asked me as we dragged one of the small rowboats off the beach and into the water. We had to row out to where the sailboats bobbed, tied to a big blue float. Next we were supposed to transfer ourselves from one boat to another, then sail the Sunfish farther into the harbor, around a marker, and back to the float.

Easy-peasy . . . except—

"They don't have sailboats in the Y pool."

"Do what I tell you and we'll pass," he said. I hopped in, awkwardly flopping into the bottom. Mr. Fuentes waved at us from the dock. I picked up an oar. Chris gave us another shove, water up to his chest, and heaved himself over the gunwale. The boat barely rocked.

"Follow my lead. We can pretend we're pirates."

"Ha-ha," I said. "Show me how to row."

Chris leaned back and forth slightly with the movement of the oars. After a few attempts where my oars just skimmed the surface of the water, I got it.

And immediately felt it in my shoulders and back. And in my hands, as they started to chafe against the wood.

I decided that I didn't like rowing.

Thankfully, a few strokes later we pulled up next to the float. Chris had me raise my oars and he piloted us in like Luke navigating the canyons of the Death Star.

It surprised me that Chris knew how to handle a boat—most city kids don't. He pulled us next to one of the small Sunfishes and unclipped the line at the bow, then attached it to our rowboat.

"Hold the sailboat," he directed. I grabbed on.

Next, he pulled himself into the sailboat, which rocked. I held tight, feeling like my arm was going to pop out of its socket. Chris carefully reached into the bottom of the boat, where I couldn't see. He came up with a board with a thicker piece attached to the top, which he dropped into a slot. He grabbed the rowboat.

"It's stable. Come over," he said.

I heaved myself from one boat to the other.

"This is stable?" The whole thing felt like it was going to flip over. I sat, very still, on one of the benches while Chris untied lines, handed me one, and stuck my hand on the rudder.

"Hold the line tight and pull when I tell you. It'll raise the sail, and we don't need it up until we get away from the float. Keep the rudder straight." He guided us out of our parking spot by hand, pushing us away from the other boats.

"Did you learn all this at summer camp?" Every other team I'd watched had landed in the water by now, either tipping their sailboat or falling when crossing from the rowboat to the Sunfish.

"The city of Boston offers sailing classes on the Charles for a dollar," he said. He took the rudder from me. "My mom signs me up every summer because she thinks I should be outside. I really like it, but it's not as fun as camp. Pull the line."

I tugged and the sail slid up the mast. It caught the wind and I felt the strength of it in my aching shoulder.

"Wrap the cleat!" Chris called out. "You can't hold it!" For a second, I didn't know what he meant. I turned to look for the cleat he was talking about, and the sail slackened. The boat lurched.

"Pull!"

I pulled, then saw the cleat he was referring to. I wrapped the rope around it in a figure eight pattern, making sure to keep it taut the whole time. The boat picked up speed, and we slid through the water toward the marker.

Something didn't seem right, and it took me a minute to put my finger on it.

Chris was *quiet*. And he'd been giving *directions*, not just asking questions.

I snuck a peek over my shoulder. He held on to the rudder, looking ahead to the marker, grinning from ear to ear. This was the same kid whose motormouth could power the T? This kid was so relaxed he looked like he was born on the water. I shook my head, trying not to smile. The breeze across the water shifted, and the sail snapped.

"Boom!" Chris yelled.

I turned to him, and *whack!* got smacked in the back of the head from the—duh—boom.

"Ow!" I cried, and ducked, late. The sail cracked like a whip and pivoted to the other side of the mast.

"You okay?" Chris asked. "I yelled to warn you."

"'Boom!' is not a warning," I pointed out. "It's the noise something makes when it explodes."

"It's also the part of the boat that's swinging past your noggin," he replied. "Boom!"

Smack! The bar hit me again. I ducked.

"Seriously?!" This was going to leave a mark.

Chris laughed. "Dude! You need to duck!"

"Figured that out, Captain," I replied.

We rounded the marker, Chris yelling "Boom!" two more times. The third time, I didn't hear the sail snap. I peeked up at him, and he was cracking up.

"The boom didn't swing, did it?"

"Nah. Just messin' with you."

The float, with the attached boats, bobbed like some strange water lily. Chris pulled the sail down and reversed the process of guiding us in: Clip the line from the rowboat to the sailboat, hang on, stow gear, switch boats.

And row back to shore.

Lucky for my back and shoulders, the waves helped us along.

"Yo ho, yo ho, a pirate's life for me!" Chris sang as we hit the beach.

15

It seemed like we were spending all day on the water. When the rest of the scouts finished their water safety tests, they were dismissed and told that they'd spend the hour before dinner playing Manhunt.

"Not you two." Mr. Fuentes snagged Chris and me as we left the beach. "Ranger Johnson asked if you could return to Gallops Island with him, because he was dissatisfied with your work yesterday. What were you boys doing?"

Chris and I exchanged glances. So *this* was how he was going to get us over there. Awesome.

"Sorry, sir," Chris said. "We got to fooling around, and then Ollie got hurt, and so we never completed our assignment."

Mr. Fuentes was *not* happy. "Go. Work. I'm telling him not to bring you back for dinner until that wall is repaired to his satisfaction. And instead of your regular chores, you're on trash duty tonight. Understand?"

We nodded.

Chris and I took off in opposite directions. He headed up to the tent to change, and I decided to loop over to the dock first, to see if Ranger Johnson could at least put us on Mr. Fuentes's good side again.

I stayed in the shade on the way to the dock. Before I came out of the trees, I heard an agitated voice in front of me.

"I don't have them yet," it grumbled. "I don't know when I will—taking two of the runts over there later to look—but you can bet I won't just sit on them when I do get them."

Ranger Johnson. The hair on the back of my neck prickled. This was *not* good.

"Listen, I'll let you know. You'll have your piece. I'm good for it. No. Not a problem. They think they're going to a *museum*." He cackled at that one. Then: silence.

Burned and angry, I didn't know what was going on, but I did know two things:

I was not handing over any treasure to Ranger Johnson.

I needed to contact Agent Goh.

Oh, make that three:

I was not doing well at staying out of trouble.

The speedboat, nearly empty, bounced over the waves. Ranger Johnson opened up the throttle in the short distance between the two islands.

"We're going to find *treaaaassssssuuure!*" he howled into the wind. Chris whooped and cheered as the boat slammed over the waves. I offered a weak smile, hoping they would think I was seasick more than anything else.

"Anything else" meaning being worried sick.

I hadn't had a chance to tell Chris what I'd heard, so he still thought we were Indiana Jones–ing the treasure, instead of playing the part of the bad guys. We had to get to the cave and check out the rocks without Ranger Johnson finding the location—while we were the only three people on the island. This was not going to be easy. The boat crossed a particularly big wave, and my teeth clacked together as the plume of sea spray swept back at us.

Thankfully, we reached the No Wake Zone quickly. Ranger Johnson cut the speed and Chris played the part of Derek, hopping out and tying the boat to the cleats while Ranger Johnson guided it close to the dock.

I racked my brain. How was I going to do this?

Ranger Johnson cut the engine and climbed out.

"Need a hand, Dad?"

Grey.

"What are you doing here?" the ranger demanded. His face turned a dull brick color. "This island isn't safe!"

Grey waved one hand dismissively. "Heard you might need some help with the team," she said, tossing a glance in my direction. "And I was here the other day. It was safe enough then." I didn't even care that I'd been thrown under the bus for the second time this afternoon. Her presence meant Chris and I had a shot of getting into that cave.

Ranger Johnson and his daughter bickered for another minute or so, while my mind raced through possibilities. Could I send them somewhere else? Fake sick? Use Chris to distract the ranger and go to the cave with Grey? The ranger addressed the three of us before I could come to any conclusions.

"Okay. So, we don't have a lot of time. There are a few sites that Derek and I didn't get to the other day, so I thought we could split them up." He brought out a map with three locations X'ed off.

X marks the spot? I almost laughed at how absurd this was, but was too stressed. Then I saw past the shiny.

"Two of these are close to where Chris and I were the other day, sir," I pointed out. "Why don't we check there, and you and Grey can check . . ." I ran my finger to the farthest X on the island—almost exactly opposite from where Chris and I would be, on a hill on the far side of the island. "Here?"

Grey scowled at me, like she knew I was trying to get rid of her—and I kind of was—but I needed her to keep the ranger away from the cave.

"All right," the ranger said grudgingly. "I suppose we can't all go together if we're going to cover the largest amount of area." I tried to hide the relief I felt. He went on to tell us to be aware that the treasure was probably buried or tucked into something—a hollow of a tree, for instance.

Seriously? X marks the spot and hollow trees? No way anything is lasting three hundred years in a hollow tree—even I know that. Was Ranger Johnson pulling some elaborate joke? Was I on one of those prank shows or something?.

"Ollie's got great eyes for finding stuff," Chris said. I was grateful that his enthusiasm masked my complete lack of faith in this guy.

We set a report time—we had barely an hour—and split up. Not before I caught Grey's narrow-eyed glare.

I'd programmed the coordinates into my GPS before we left, so it wasn't long before we were sliding over the berm and into the cave.

Chris clicked the flashlight on and shined it into the hole. There they were: rocks—dozens of them—on the floor of the cubby.

"Are those . . . ?" Chris trailed off. I stuck my bandaged arm through the hole again, and grabbed a fistful. When I opened it, about ten rocks, ranging from SuperBall to pea-sized, gave off a dusty sparkle.

"Um," said Chris, at a loss for words for once.

"Yeah," I said, gulping. "I think they are."

Neither of us wanted to say the word:

Jewels. But what kinds?

We stood, staring. Chris took a few out of my hand and clicked them together. I filled him in on the phone call that I'd overheard, and my suspicions about the ranger.

"So we didn't find these?" Chris asked.

"Exactly," I said. "You never even saw the cave." I told him that I planned to ask Dr. Gupta for his cell phone, so I could call the FBI and figure out what to do next.

"Of *course* you can just call the FBI!" Chris cracked up.

"Lay off."

"No! It's cool," he said. "C'mon, Ollie, how many kids can just call the FBI to find out what to do with pirate treasure?

He had a point.

"What about Grey?" he asked. "She's on our team."

This was the not-cool part. "Team or not, I don't think we can tell her yet," I said slowly. "I'm not sure I trust her to keep this from her dad. Let me talk to the FBI before we talk to her." He agreed.

There was no way to take all of the . . . rocks . . . out of the cave. We'd need a bag, or, if we used our pockets, we'd have to explain why they were bulging. Together, we decided that the best thing to do was to leave most of them where they were.

"But we need to hide them again," I pointed out.

Chris untied the long-sleeve T-shirt he'd been wearing around his waist, balled it up, and dredged it through the sand and muck at our feet. Next, he stuffed it in the hole. It wasn't well camouflaged, but hopefully no one would come in here looking for lost outerwear. And hopefully Grey wouldn't wonder why we'd stuffed the shirt in the hole. I dropped a few . . . rocks . . . in one of the pockets of my cargo shorts.

We climbed out of the cave, dusted off, and consulted the map for where we were actually supposed to be on the island. We cruised by the spots—nothing to see, just scrubby grass and trees—and went back to the dock.

Ranger Johnson and Grey were waiting for us.

We were still a distance from them when Ranger Johnson called, "Anything?"

I shook my head and held up empty palms. *But I have a handful of treasure in my pocket!* The voice in my head screamed with anxiety. I hoped Chris could hold it together.

"You guys?" I asked when we got closer. They shook their heads.

"We'll try again," the ranger promised. "I think the spots you had are more promising, but might require digging."

My pockets are promising! I thought. This was crazy. I had who knew how many thousands of dollars of what might be jewels clicking around in a pair of cargo shorts.

What would happen if I fell out of the boat? Or tripped? Or if there was a hole in my pocket? Sweat broke out across my back.

Chris unwound the cleats and we climbed into the boat. As we bounced back to Lovells, I suddenly realized that Grey hadn't spoken. When I looked at her she was staring straight at me, stormy eyes boiling.

She didn't need to say a word.

DAY 8

CHRIS'S GOTCHA! ALIVE/TAGGED LIST

STEVE

D-BAG DEREK

~~ME (CHRIS)~~

JACK

MANNY

~~DOUG~~

PETE

~~HORATIO~~

CAM

~~JORGE~~

RAVI

OLLIE

16

"Do you hear anything?" Jack asked for the six thousandth time. Steve hadn't exacted his revenge for the pee incident yet, and Jack's paranoia was making all of us jumpy.

Okay, the "rocks" Chris and I were hiding didn't help either.

"Dude, we're in our *tent*. No Gotcha! play allowed here, although it would be really cool if we could do it," Chris whispered. He yawned. "Give it up and go to sleep."

"If you guys get me caught tonight, I'll—"

"You'll, what, Manny?" I said. He was prepping for his midnight swim.

He threw his balled-up sweatshirt at me. "I'll . . . be really mad," he finished.

"Can I go with you?" Chris was already wearing his trunks and rolling his towel.

"Just don't get me caught!" Manny warned.

"Let's all go," I said, surprising myself. I don't know where the idea came from—thanks to the salt water during the boating test, parts of my scratched-up arm had developed a nice yellowish ooze—but all of a sudden going for a swim in the middle of the night seemed like the thing to do. It was *normal*—what kids are supposed to do at camp.

"Are you crazy?" Jack asked. "The second you guys leave I'll be dead."

"First, you said you didn't care what Steve would do to get his revenge, because your prank was so good," I pointed out, "and second, come with us and you won't be alone."

"And third: You won't get a sunburn," Chris offered. Jack actually nodded at that one.

"Aw, man," Manny said. "All right. Let's do this."

I wasn't sure Jack was going to go for it. He sat on top of his sleeping bag, watching us while we got our stuff together. Then, without a word, he got up and grabbed his suit.

"Here." Manny tossed me the bug spray, and I doused my back and shoulders and tossed it to Chris. I'd stuffed my contraband-holding cargo shorts in the bottom of my sleeping bag. I checked to make sure they were still there. Manny pulled back the torn flap of the tent, motioned for us to be quiet, and we slipped out, one at a time.

We didn't speak as we left the camping area. Two of the tents leaked light around the edges of their flaps. We weren't the only ones up.

The walk from the campsite to the beach wasn't long, but the path was bumpy and Manny refused to let us use flashlights. Finally, though, we crested the ridge where we'd seen the porpoises, and went down the far side to the beach.

Instead of heading for the flat, open section of the sand, Manny led us to one side, where shadows stretched out to the water. He stashed his T-shirt and towel behind a rock, and we did the same. A cool breeze prickled my skin.

"Let's go!" Manny raced to the water, Chris right behind him. I didn't run as fast—my legs and back were still aching from my experience with the rowboat, then trekking around Gallops.

The calm water splashed over my feet. I waded out, shaking off the chill, and dove. When I came up, Jack was near me, head dripping and skin so white he glowed.

Manny splashed us, and that started a whole splash fight.

Finally, when we were all spluttering and cold, Chris called a truce.

We slogged back to the beach and dried off.

On the walk back, Jack whispered, "Did you just hear that?"

"I'm gonna start calling you Paranoia instead of Whiz," Manny responded. "There's nothing—" But then we all heard it: a rustling, snapping noise from the trees.

We froze. Then, from Chris, "Run!"

Gotcha! time. We took off toward camp, and safety. Chris was already out, and we knew Steve had Jack. I couldn't see who was behind us, but I heard his footsteps. Heart pounding, I veered off the path and into the trees. Manny went straight. The kid chasing us came after me.

Crud.

Steel bands clamped around my chest; my heart slammed. Stupid inhaler was back in the tent. This kid would catch me for sure.

Ahead of me was the opening in the tree line for the campsite. I willed my legs to move faster. The guy behind me was gaining ground.

My foot clomped on a thick tree branch, which rolled underneath it. I lost my balance and went flying—arms out, face-first, right into the dirt. My glasses popped off.

It's over. I'm dead.

I flipped over to see who was after me. Cam—the destroyer—was steps away, arms extended, red "kill" sticker balanced on the end of his finger. Without thinking, I stuck my foot out, tripping him. He went down much the same way I had: arms and legs out, flying across the ground.

I grabbed my glasses, hopped up, my lungs feeling like they were sized for a squirrel, and wheezed past him. Steps away from the campsite, he was behind me again. I came out of the trees behind the tent next to ours barely ahead of him, and grabbed its nylon sides.

"Safe," I said, only it came out as a breathy whoosh.

"This time," Cam growled. His T-shirt was smeared with dirt, just like mine.

I wheezed some more, and dropped my hands to my knees and tilted my head back, trying to get more air into my lungs.

"You okay?" he asked.

I couldn't talk any more. My lungs had shrunk to chipmunk size and the Very Bad Gray Cloud was at the edges of my vision. I tried to stay calm, but the only sounds were the rush of blood in my ears and the squeaking coming from my chest.

This was Pass Out Land.

I closed my eyes.

Something pushed into my mouth. Something hard and plastic.

My inhaler! I didn't even open my eyes, just pushed the

plunger hard and sucked in as much of the medicine as I could into my tiny lungs.

The medicine cloud tasted like licorice and felt like heaven. I held it in for as long as I could, blew it out, and immediately pressed the plunger again. Technically, I wasn't supposed to do two puffs, but this was an emergency. Whoever brought me my inhaler probably grabbed my regular one, not the super-injector rescue inhaler in the bottom of my pack. The steel bands around my chest finally loosened. Eyes still closed, I coughed and leaned my head back and just tried to breathe, waiting for the pain to go away and my lungs to grow back to their natural size.

"Ollie? Ollie? You okay, dude? Is he okay? Guys, do you think he's fine? He won't open his eyes. Ollie—can you open your eyes? Hey, Ollie, c'mon . . ."

Chris's motormouth was getting on my nerves.

I opened my eyes. Chris was nearly nose to nose with me. I pushed against the tree.

"His eyes are open! He's okay! Dude, you scared the snot out of me. I thought we were going to have to get the helicopter to get you off the island. Which would be cool, but you know, not really, 'cause it'd be you in it, but it would be cool for the rest of us who would get to see a rescue copter in action . . ."

Chris went on, and I closed my eyes again. Had they told Mr. Fuentes and Dr. Gupta? My coughing and wheezing was so loud, I'd probably woken the whole camp. And if I had, and the parent leaders found out about Gotcha! everyone in the tent would hate me.

It almost made me wish for helicopter rescue.

Chris, Jack, Manny, and Cam hovered around the tree and me. We waited for my breathing to ease up and for the coughs to stop. My back hurt from the spasms.

A flashlight clicked on and Chris's and Jack's faces lit like a freaky Halloween party trick.

"What's going on?" Mr. Fuentes said. The light swung my way.

"Ollie had an asthma attack on his way to the latrine," Chris said. "He left the tent and didn't come back and we heard this noise, like an engine, ya know? And so Jack and Manny went to check it out and then they saw Ollie. They were freaked out . . ."

I went from being annoyed by Chris's continuous chatter to grateful for it. Mr. Fuentes turned to him.

"So why did you stay in the tent?"

Chris hung his head and did a half shrug. "I was too scared to go out. But then Jack came back and told me something was wrong with Ollie, and he uses an inhaler, so I grabbed it off his sleeping bag and we came out here."

My breathing was back to normal, but I knew better than to say anything. I just waited while Chris lied through his teeth for me.

"Are you okay?" Mr. Fuentes crouched down next to me. I nodded. I didn't want to talk too much, just in case it brought the coughs back.

"Tired," I said. It wasn't a lie. An asthma attack wipes me out. All I wanted was sleep. I'd even put my head on a rock.

"Let's get you back to your tent," Mr. Fuentes said. "You seem okay for the time being. We'll discuss calling your parents in the morning."

I was too exhausted to even protest.

17

When I woke up, the inside of the tent was bright and sticky-hot, and my head and back throbbed. I was so thirsty, it felt like I hadn't had anything to drink since I landed on the island.

I guzzled the lukewarm water left in my bottle, tugged on shorts and a shirt, and stepped outside.

The campsite was silent and totally empty. No one by the fire pit, no one hanging around. I'd left my watch in the tent, but by checking the sun, I guessed it was somewhere around ten—totally respectable for sleeping in at home on vacation, but a "wasted day" according to Wilderness Scout camp rules. I couldn't remember the day's schedule, but guessed some scouts would be at the beach or down by the fort.

I did remember that Mr. Fuentes wanted to talk to me.

Great.

I refilled my water bottle from the camp cooler, then found my Sox hat and inhaler and headed to the beach.

Mr. Fuentes was down there, supervising a bunch of guys who were working on lifesaving skills. Chris was in the group, and he waved at me as I approached. Mr. Fuentes turned around.

"Good morning," he said. "How are you feeling?"

There was no way I was going to tell him about my headache.

"Okay. Sorry I slept so late. Big asthma attacks wear me out." I picked my words carefully, in case he was waiting for a reason to send me home.

"Let's sit down." Mr. Fuentes pointed at a bench a few yards away from the pier.

I sat and took my hat off, to have something to do with my hands while we talked.

"Ollie, I think you're a good kid. And a great scout." I gulped. If he sent me home, then what would happen? Agent Goh wanted me out of the city for a minimum of two weeks while his team did their work and the media frenzy died down. What would I do? What would my family do? Both of my parents worked, and it was hard for them to take time off without planning it. Even the additional $2.5 million in my bank account wouldn't help. They insisted that money would be for "college and beyond" and we weren't to touch it.

"It's just . . ." He faltered for a moment, like he didn't know what to say next. "It's just, I'm not sure this is a good place for you. You keep running into . . . challenges. And, frankly, I'm afraid that your parents will be very upset with me if I return you to them in this condition."

Okay. This kind of worry I could deal with.

"It's okay," I responded. "Seriously. My asthma gets crazy all the time. It's not a big deal." I hope-hope-hoped that he bought my lie. Because my asthma *did* get crazy, but not like this. Last night's episode had been the worst one in a while, and that was saying something. "I really like it here. I like the guys in the troop, and what happened on Gallops Island was an accident. My arm is much better now than it was two days ago, even. See?"

I held it up. The punctures and scratches had scabbed over, and although they weren't pretty, it no longer looked as though a mountain lion had been using it as a scratching post. I hoped it was enough to get him to agree, because if I got sent home, what would happen to the rocks?

Briefly, I considered telling him about our find, but I was pretty sure that would land me straight on a boat home. Plus, once you got burned the way I had by the restoration guy from the Gardner, you don't want to tell anyone anything ever again. No, I couldn't tell him.

Mr. Fuentes dropped his head to his hands, then rubbed them briskly back and forth over his scalp. "You're killing me," he said.

"Don't call them, okay? I promise I'll carry my rescue inhaler around all the time," I said. "You can spot check me for it. And I won't run so much," I added as an afterthought. Even though running didn't necessarily make my asthma worse—*being chased* did.

"There's less than one week left, Ollie. Anything else happens to you—a hangnail, a cold, *anything*—I am calling them. No more discussion. And you need to take better care of yourself out here. Got it?"

"Absolutely." I raised my hand and grinned. "Scout's honor."

Mr. Fuentes let me take off the morning activities—he wanted me to lay low at the campsite. I knew exactly how I'd spend my time.

Before I left the beach I filled a pail with water, then went back to my tent and dredged the bottom of my sleeping bag for my cargo shorts.

I poured the "rocks" into my hand. I'd only grabbed a handful from the cave, in case they were just rocks. I hoped Chris would forgive me for doing this without him, but we'd waited too long already. And I had to know if they were real before I called Agent Goh.

Digging through my pack, I found an old toothbrush that I'd stuck in an inside pocket. I used it to dust off the fasteners on some of the metal canisters in outdoor caches. If they get grimy, they can rust and be hard to open. Next, I dropped the rocks in the pail of water and rubbed the bristles of the toothbrush across my bar of soap, then picked up a rock and scrubbed.

Cleaned of a couple hundred years of grime, it didn't look like a rock anymore. Neither did the others. They pooled in my hands like tiny ice cubes, only warm instead of cold. And worth way more money.

A chill ran down my back.

This was for real: diamonds.

I sat there, just looking at them. I pinched one between two fingers, took it to the tent flap, and held it to the sun.

It was half as big as the thumb drive I used to transfer my work between the computer lab at school and home, and kind of a square shape with round corners. My mom's engagement ring from my dad was a diamond, and when she washed it before going out, it glinted like crazy. She told me that's because it has facets on it—flat sides and angles that make the light reflect and bounce around. If the angle of the sun was right, sometimes when we were inside she could make a "star" zip around the room from the reflection from her ring. LeeLee loved it. She'd chase it. Thinking about them gave me a tiny twinge of homesickness.

But this diamond didn't have many facets—just a flat front and back, and slanty edges on the sides. It didn't sparkle very much.

What if they weren't real? How would I know? I'd look like an idiot if I called the FBI and told them I found diamonds, thought the park ranger was up to something, and they turned out to be fakes. I had to figure out how be sure.

And since I wasn't, yet, I had to put them away. I rummaged around the tent and found an empty aluminum mints tin. The diamonds rattled around inside, but when I lined it with (clean) bandages, they were silent. I tucked the tin deep into a pocket of my shorts, cleaned up my mess, and tried to figure out what to do with the maybe-diamonds.

Here's how you get in trouble with your scoutmaster:

Break a promise to take care of yourself barely three hours after making it.

Pete was back in camp society, and I'd decided that I'd had enough of people coming after me—I wanted to be on the other side of the chasing. We'd been on a nature and tracking hike, identifying different species on the island for a Parks Department census. His bandages were off and the oozing had stopped.

The hike wound up at the top of the hill overlooking the beach, and Ranger Johnson turned to us.

"This is where I leave you, guys. I need to collect your sheets. Thanks from the Parks Department." I held out my mini clipboard and pen. We'd divided a parcel of the island into sections with a scout responsible for each. I'd seen six rabbits and two seagulls. By the looks on the faces of the five other guys on the hike, they hadn't seen anything any more exciting.

Pete handed his stuff over to the ranger and headed in the direction of camp. Ranger Johnson took my clipboard and I was about to follow Pete, when the ranger cleared his throat.

"Could you wait a minute please, Ollie?"

I turned.

"How's the arm?"

"Better," I said. I stuck it out for him to look at, then got ready to walk away.

"That was a nasty fall you took," he said, barely looking at the scratches. "I'm pretty sure there were a dozen splinters in there that had to come out."

I nodded, suddenly realizing how alone we were and how uncomfortable that felt.

"How did you fall again?"

My chest tightened—just a little, but enough of a reminder from last night. I gulped. This guy was rattling me.

"Off the embankment," I answered. "Just leaned over too far." *Keep the lie simple*, I told myself. *It's more believable that way.*

Ranger Johnson inspected the nails on his left hand. "I doubt it," he said mildly. "And I don't think you checked the site I sent you to on Gallops yesterday."

His words, although not threatening, sent a chill through my body that rivaled a brisk March day. Had Grey told him where we were? Or what we'd found?

I stayed silent. I hadn't done anything wrong—except lie.

"Wanna know how I know?" He leaned down a little to talk to me and I caught a whiff of sweat and cologne. My stomach flipped. All of a sudden, I had the sensation of déjà vu—I'd heard of it, but hadn't really ever had it before. All the hair on my body stood on end. I couldn't move. I definitely couldn't speak.

"I *know*," he continued, probably giving up on me responding, "because if you fell off the embankment above the retaining wall, you'd have landed on the *beach*. In *sand*. And you'd have bruises. This"—he gestured to my arm—"*this* is not from sand.

"And don't tell me that you landed on driftwood. You'd have impaled yourself and collapsed a lung, not had splinters to remove from one arm. And I know you didn't spend time at the site yesterday because you would have found *this*," he barked, holding out a tarnished coin. "So I'll ask you *one more time*. Where were you?"

That last part was delivered through clenched teeth. Any tiny bit of belief that Ranger Johnson was just a normal guy doing his job disappeared faster than a drop of blood in the ocean: This was not good. I was pretty sure he'd planted that coin as a way to test Chris and me.

We'd failed.

I swallowed, hoping my airway would stay open and that

someone would come to the top of the hill and rescue me. But if there was anything that I learned this summer, it's that most of the time, you're the only one who can rescue yourself.

"You're right," I said, hoping to buy myself a little time. "But I didn't find anything. And I didn't fall off the retaining wall. Chris and I were horsing around when it happened and I didn't want to get in trouble."

While I spoke, my brain reviewed the terrain on Gallops Island.

"We decided to go to one of the ruins—the mess hall, I think?—anyway, there's a wooden fence there, with the No Trespassing sign on it. Chris dared me to tag the sign, and when I jumped up to do it, I knocked it off the post and fell on it. This arm was underneath me, which is how I got the scratches. And we didn't check the spot that carefully yesterday. I was tired from the swimming and boating—I'm not used to it—so we just walked around instead of looking hard."

I hung my head. "I'm really sorry."

I waited, hoping that he bought the story that sat sour in my mouth.

When I looked up again, he was still staring straight at me, eyes hard. "Maybe," he said. "You'd better be telling me the truth, or you're on the next boat to Boston."

I didn't look away, but didn't speak. It was an easy lie to catch me in: If the sign had been knocked off the post and broken, I was in the clear. If not, he'd be coming for more information.

And of course the sign was in perfect condition.

He stood and stalked off toward the camp. I remained standing in the same spot, waiting. Thinking.

Before Ranger Johnson found out what I'd been up to and had me sent home, I had to get back to Gallops.

Fast.

18

I gave Ranger Johnson a head start, then I tried really, really hard not to run back to camp. Instead, I half ran, half walked. Speed walked, if you will.

I had to get back to Gallops as soon as possible and take that sign down—like, tonight. I didn't know how I'd get over there, but Chris and I would figure it out.

Because if Ranger Johnson found out the truth—that we had the diamonds and lied to him—I'd be in big trouble. The only person who could help me out of it was somewhere in Boston, overseeing one of the biggest criminal investigations in the city's history.

But wait—I had a way out of this after all: Dr. Gupta! It was easy.

I just had to call Agent Goh on Dr. Gupta's cell phone.

Feeling lighter, I beelined for the campsite.

When I got there, though, everyone was in an uproar. Doug, who should have known better, cut himself while using his hatchet to chop firewood. There was blood all over the chopping stump, and Mr. Fuentes, Dr. Gupta, and Ranger Johnson hunched together, taking care of him while the rest of the scouts speculated in groups about what would happen.

"Medivac," said Steve. "Totally." A few guys nodded.

"Boat," said Derek. "It's not life threatening." Other guys agreed.

Chris hovered at arm's reach, offering his first aid and life-saving skills to the adults. Doug sat on a log with his hand bandaged and over his head, his face a milky white.

Mr. Fuentes stood.

"Attention," he called. We shuffled closer. My chest tightened as soon as I saw Ranger Johnson, but he didn't return my gaze.

"Dr. Gupta will take Doug to the mainland by boat, so he can go to the hospital and get a tetanus shot and his hand stitched." At this, Doug looked even worse—like he might pass out or barf. Or barf, then pass out.

"Ranger Johnson has offered to stay on site; we're going to keep you guys close."

Terror and relief raced through me. I mean, on the one hand, it was good—Ranger Johnson couldn't get to Gallops Island to check the sign I supposedly knocked over either—but on the other hand, the lifeline that I thought I had to Agent Goh and the FBI was heading to the Brigham hospital.

Ranger Johnson radioed for the Parks Department boat, and Derek and Steve were tasked with packing Doug's stuff.

Chris bounded over to me. "This is crazy, isn't it? I mean, Doug's always been all thumbs—remember the flaming marshmallow from the other night?—but he really did it this time. Last year, he nearly took out his eye running into a branch playing flashlight tag on the last night—did I tell you that we do that? It's awesome—and he had this big red stink eye. So gross!

But he's never done anything this stupid. I swear, he nearly cut his fingers off."

I nodded in all the right places.

"Listen, Chris," I said, keeping my voice low and barely moving my mouth. "I have to tell you something."

I give the kid credit: He may be a high-energy motormouth, but he caught my wave.

"What's up?"

"The ranger is onto us, and it's not cool. We have to get back to Gallops." I told him I'd give him the details when we had some space. He nodded, and although the questions were written all over his face, the only thing he said was "Cool."

Ranger Johnson, Dr. Gupta, and Mr. Fuentes stayed by Doug's side until the dock radioed that the boat had come in. The three adults helped Doug down to the boat. Derek carried his stuff. Chris and I were hanging outside our tent, playing cards with Jack and Manny when they went by, and the ranger shot me a look that had "I'm watching you" all over it.

I expected to be scared, but instead I felt challenged.

"Let's do this," I whispered.

Once Doug was on the boat, Ranger Johnson and Mr. F. snapped us into action. They didn't want us to "waste daylight," they said, and had us spend the hours before dinner clearing debris from some of the island paths and picking up trash. It was like they wanted to tire us out so we'd be too exhausted to get into any trouble.

"Trash pickup is my least favorite community service," Chris said as we grabbed garbage sticks and headed toward one of the paths. I talked while we walked and explained that I'd cleaned the "rocks" and thought we might have something. I also told him about my weird conversation with Ranger Johnson about my arm.

"Why do you think Ranger Johnson is so interested in your arm?" he asked. "I mean, it doesn't really matter how it happened, but he's making it into such a big deal. Do you think it's because of Grey? She said he's one of those freaky protective dads who doesn't let their kid do anything. But that's weird, because she has her own boat. You don't give a kid her own boat if you think she's going to disappear when you're not looking at her." He paused for a breath. Maybe he was onto something.

"Has he said anything to *you* about my arm?" I stabbed a stray Dunkin' Donuts cup and dropped it in the garbage bag.

"No, dude. Nothing. Which is weird, 'cause I was with you the whole time. But maybe he asked Grey. She was there too. He could've found out stuff from her that we don't know about. I haven't seen her in a while, though. Have you?"

"Uh-uh," I said. "And it's making me nervous. She's a wild card." Chris held his bag open and I dropped in a disgusting sandwich wrapper.

"What if she told her dad?" he asked.

I'd been thinking the same thing.

"I don't think she did, because he would've said something to me today. He has no idea that we found something. She might *think* we have something, but she doesn't want to say anything to him yet."

"Right. Right. So we can call the FBI now, and get them involved, right? They'll come over here and take care of the ranger and we'll be good to go, right?"

"Whoa!" I had to stop him. "Chill. Dr. Gupta took Doug to the mainland. He has the phone." Well, the only phone I felt comfortable asking to use. I suppose I could ask Mr. Fuentes, but he already thought I was a mess—what if he used the phone call as an excuse to send me home on the next boat? Then, not only would Agent Goh be annoyed that I was home early, but I'd leave Chris alone to deal with the rest of the diamonds—and the ranger.

Chris leaned against his garbage stick, considering my point.

"Okay," he said finally. He sighed and stabbed at a piece of trash. "So now what?"

As soon as he said that, instead of relief, the pressure around my chest grew.

Forget my sidekick status. Like it or not, I was the leader in this situation. I took a breath.

"First, we have to figure out whether or not the rocks are actually what we think they are."

"And then?"

"I think we're going to have to go back to Gallops. Alone."

DAY 9

CHRIS'S GOTCHA! ALIVE/TAGGED LIST

STEVE

D-BAG DEREK

~~ME (CHRIS)~~

JACK

MANNY

~~DOUG~~ (left camp)

PETE

~~HORATIO~~

CAM

~~JORGE~~

RAVI

OLLIE

19

Ranger Johnson patrolled back and forth from our tent to Derek and Steve's. Did he think we were going to sneak out? Did Mr. Fuentes know he was doing this?

At first, it freaked us out, but by a little after twelve, Manny was getting antsy and the rest of us were still wide-awake. I couldn't sleep knowing the ranger was just outside of my tent— and I think the other guys felt the same way. Ranger Johnson was targeting me—and my friends—because he thought I was hiding something from him.

He was right, but still.

"I can't break my streak," Manny whispered to us. We knew Ranger Johnson could hear us through the not-quite walls, so we had to lie still and not say anything until we heard his footsteps head toward Derek's tent, two rows away from ours.

"Dude, you are so dead," Jack said. "Don't do it."

"Is it worth getting caught?" I added. Actually, it might be. At first, I thought Manny should just skip it and stay in. Streaks break all the time, big deal. But the more I thought about it, Manny hadn't done anything wrong—according to what Ranger Johnson actually knew, *none* of us had—so why was he patrolling our tents? Dr. Gupta and Mr. Fuentes *never* did this.

"Go for it," I whispered. The other guys stared at me like they had laser eyes. "We'll cover for you."

Manny grinned. Together, we hatched a quick plan: Manny and Chris would sneak out of our tent the next time Ranger Johnson left for Derek's. Manny'd swim, Chris would hide in the tree line shadows as a lookout. If Ranger Johnson saw him, he'd pretend he needed to visit the latrine. Jack and I would stay inside in case he stuck his head in.

We stuffed Chris's and Manny's laundry into their sleeping bags. It wasn't sculptural genius, but the results were passably lumpy. We waited.

Ranger Johnson clomped back to our tent. We quieted down.

Just then, from somewhere outside came a series of loud pops.

The sound scared the noodles out of me and probably everyone else in the camp. I jumped. Jack grabbed Chris, and Manny hit the deck. Ranger Johnson shouted and ran toward the noise, which, a second later, we realized was from firecrackers.

We laughed at our silly reactions, then left the tent—along with every other scout. Guys were milling around by the dying fire, and Ranger Johnson and Mr. Fuentes were shouting for order.

"Now's your chance," I said to Manny. Smart kid went back into our tent and out the rip in the back.

"Enough nonsense! Everyone back to bed," Mr. Fuentes called. His tent was across from ours, on the other side of the fire. He looked like he was about go back into it, when Ranger Johnson crossed over to him and whispered in his ear. We couldn't hear them, but it was clear from Mr. F.'s posture that whatever the ranger said was completely annoying.

"This is a serious offense," Ranger Johnson said. "Fireworks are illegal in Massachusetts, and we need to know who was responsible for this."

"Ranger Johnson will talk to each of you guys tonight," Mr. F. said, then he disappeared back into his tent.

Jack, Chris, and I ducked into our tent, but not before I caught Derek, Steve, and Cam elbowing one another. Derek saw me watching them, and gave me a death glare.

We sat on our sleeping bags in the dark, waiting for Manny to get back, and listening to Ranger Johnson tromp all over camp. Chris, Jack, and I figured it out at the same time: He was going tent to tent, asking about the firecrackers.

"We're dead," Jack said. "So dead."

"Manny's really dead," I pointed out. "We're sorta dead."

"We can cover for him," Chris said. "We have to."

I agreed, but I couldn't see a way out of this. The streak would break and Manny would be in big, big trouble. With the way things had gone at camp this week, Mr. Fuentes would have Manny on the mainland before lunchtime—do not pass Go, do not collect $200.

There weren't that many tents in our camp. What felt like a second later, Ranger Johnson was at the one nearest us. We could hear him talking to the guys inside: Did they know who did this? Had they been in their tent all night?

Across from me, Jack glowed palely in the little bit of moonlight that seeped in through the thin walls. He held his hand up: fingers crossed. I nodded and did the same. So did Chris.

A rustle, followed by a tight zipper. Ranger Johnson left the tent next to ours.

His footsteps crunched. He stopped in front of our "door."

Manny still wasn't back.

My heart raced, and the familiar tightness clamped around my chest. I took a hit off my inhaler.

"Boys," Ranger Johnson called out, "can I come in?"

He sounded just like the Big Bad Wolf from Little Red Riding Hood, and I fought an almost uncontrollable urge to laugh and reply, "Not by the hair of our chinny chin chins."

Instead, I exhaled. Were Chris or Jack going to say anything? What if he decided to search our tent? Would he find the tin?

"Boys?" A little more sharply. "Are you in there?" The tent flap rustled, like he was going to let himself in.

"Just a minute!" squeaked Chris.

Ranger Johnson sighed in the irritated way my mom does when I ask too many questions or LeeLee demands a snack but rejects everything she's offered.

Chris crossed the tent to Manny's sleeping bag. I couldn't see him, but he was definitely messing with it.

"Boys! I don't have all night." The tent flap shook.

I seriously knew how the three pigs felt—like they were going to throw up *and* be turned into bacon.

"Ranger!" Mr. Fuentes's voice reached us. "What's going on?"

Ranger Johnson paused, then stepped away from our tent.

146

We could hear him talking to Mr. Fuentes, but their voices were too low for us to make out what they were saying.

From the back of the tent came a telltale snap of canvas.

Manny.

"Dude!" Chis whispered. He raised his hand, and the two high-fived. Then Chris punched him in the arm. "You almost got us killed!"

Manny went to his sleeping bag and tugged a dry T-shirt over his head. "I almost got caught by Fuentes," he said, voice low.

"Boys!" This time it was Mr. Fuentes outside our tent. "Can you come out here, please?" I guess he hadn't actually gone back to bed, but had thrown clothes on or something.

We obeyed, ducking out the door and standing in line in front of the tent. Manny's hair was still wet and his shirt stuck to him in patches, but in the dark it was pretty hard to tell.

"Ranger Johnson wants to discuss the incident tonight." Mr. Fuentes had a battery-operated lantern, and its cold light made the bags under his eyes stand out. The guy had had a long day.

Chris jumped right in. "We were almost asleep, and then *rat-tat-tat-tat!* Fireworks! Salutes, I think," he said. "A *bunch*. Scared me to death. And I think Ollie almost needed his inhaler again. It was pretty funny, actually—he made this hooting noise, Ollie did—and Manny hit the deck." Mr. Fuentes raised his hand.

"Do you know who lit them off?"

All of us shook our heads.

"Okay. Go back to bed. No merit badge classes in the morning. Meeting at the fire after breakfast."

Ranger Johnson scowled at us, like he wanted to say something too, but he knew it wasn't the right time or place. I ducked in after Manny, in front of Jack, and I heard Ranger Johnson say to Mr. Fuentes, "Those boys are up to something."

"Of course they are," came Mr. Fuentes's reply. "They're boys at camp. Give it a rest."

If he only knew.

20

After breakfast, Mr. Fuentes gave the obligatory "You're all in trouble and someone should step forward and admit to what they did," speech. Of course no one was going to rat anyone else out, and he knew it. But he had to put on a good show.

"Inter-island travel is suspended for the rest of camp," he added. "Ranger Johnson and I feel that you boys aren't responsible enough for another excursion. You'll be limited to Lovells only."

So *that* was our punishment. If I hadn't seen Derek all but raise his hand and claim that he'd set the salutes off, I'd have wondered if Ranger Johnson had done it himself. It was just too convenient—Ranger Johnson suspected there was something we saw or found on Gallops that we weren't telling him about, then all of a sudden we couldn't go to the island where the diamonds were supposedly hidden. Maybe it *was* time to bring Mr. Fuentes in on everything that had been going on? I just didn't want to give the wrong person too much information. Then, instead of me fading into the background, I'd be splashed all over this story too.

No way.

Once we were dismissed, Chris and I headed to the fort. Mr.

Fuentes thought we were going to set up more orienteering sites, but really, we had stuff to discuss.

"We're doomed," said Chris. "There's no way we can get back there."

I folded a few boxes. "We'd need a boat," I agreed. "And right now, boats are not an option. And we need to find out if Grey told her dad anything about the cave."

"What cave? My cave?" Grey's voice came from inside the fort. Chris and I both jumped. One of us may have yelped.

She stepped out.

"You keep doing that!" Chris cried.

"You keep forgetting to check your surroundings," she said. "And you seem to have left something behind the last time you were on Gallops." She threw Chris's filthy T-shirt to him. He caught it.

"So, *what* is going on? Spill it."

Chris raised an eyebrow and shrugged at me. I didn't trust her, but there was no way out of this situation unless I gave her *some* information. I dug around in my cargo shorts pocket for the mints tin, opened it, and picked up the largest diamond and held it to the sun. It glinted and winked in the direct light.

"Whoa," said Grey. "Where were they? The hole that your arm went through? I can't believe you didn't tell me!" She stood stiffly, arms folded, glaring. I gulped.

"There was no time," I explained. "We didn't want your dad to find out about your cave." It was a lame excuse, but the best one I had. She didn't say anything, just took one from the box. Chris did too.

"How'd you clean them?" she asked, turning hers over in her hand.

"With an old toothbrush and some soap."

"My dad is going to flip! This is Long Ben Avery's treasure!" Grey gave a for-real smile, not the big shark grin I'd gotten used to seeing, while Chris and I exchanged uneasy glances. The last person I wanted to have these was Ranger Johnson.

"We don't even know if they're real," I pointed out. "I mean, they look real, but that doesn't necessarily mean anything. My sister has play gems that shine more than these do. I'm not sure we should tell him yet."

"Are you kidding? He was the one who told you about them!"

I didn't know what to say; I was in a losing situation. I looked to Chris for help.

He bit his lip and stared at the diamond in his palm.

"I got it!" he said. "Diamonds are supposed to be super-hard, right? You cut stuff with diamonds. My dad has a diamond-tipped drill bit. What if we tested one?"

"We're not putting these on a drill!" Grey cried. "Are you crazy?"

"That's not what I mean," Chris said. "What if we scrape another rock with it? Or try to scratch it with a rock? It shouldn't leave a mark."

"Great idea," I said. "We have to know for sure, and if they break, they definitely aren't real diamonds."

Grey furrowed her eyebrows. "I'm not sure this is a good idea. Let's just give them to my dad. We're all on the same team, right?"

I avoided the question. "Look," I said, desperate. "I know you don't want to wreck them—I don't either—but we have to at least *try* to figure out if they're real. Otherwise, you guys will look like fools when we hand them over." I hoped she didn't notice my little slip.

"Okay," she said, but the word came out grudgingly.

Chris searched around the edges of the fort for a flat stone and Grey and I looked for smaller, pointier ones. We put the diamonds on the largest rock. I chose the largest diamond— the half thumb-drive-sized one—and held it tightly in my fist. Chris and Grey also grabbed one each.

"On three," I said. I took a breath. "One. Two. Three."

We dragged the diamonds across the flat gray rock. All three of them left long white lines across the stone.

"Any rock does that to another rock," Grey pointed out.

"But look at the one you're holding," I said. We all turned our diamonds over to the "point" we'd been writing with. They were perfect. Not a scratch or a mark on them.

"Watch," I said, seeing that she was still skeptical. I picked up one of the small pointy gray stones and dragged it across the larger rock. It too left a white line, but when I turned it over, the "point" I'd been writing with was also white and slightly flattened. "See?"

"Yeah." She nodded. "But this could just be a harder rock."

"*Now* who doesn't believe they're real?" I tossed back. Grey scowled at me, but she knew I was right.

Okay, there was no way to know with 100 percent certainty

that what we had was *real* pirate treasure, but I could be reasonably positive that we were holding diamonds.

The trees rustled and footsteps came from down the path.

Grey swept the diamonds off the rock and into the tin. She missed one; I snagged it and stuck it in my pocket. Chris took the tin.

"Grey! I've been looking everywhere for you."

Ranger Johnson. Crud. It was over. He was going to take the diamonds and give them to whoever he was talking to on the phone. And Chris and I would be like the young Indiana Jones who loses the Cross of Coronado at the beginning of *The Last Crusade*, instead of the Indiana Jones who defeats the Nazis and finds the Holy Grail. I prepared myself for disappointment.

Something was up with him, though. It had been a late night, sure, and he'd dealt with all the scouts yesterday, but he looked both exhausted and jittery, if that was possible.

His hands couldn't stay still. They pulled at the neck of his T-shirt, rubbed his thighs, and ran through his hair. He didn't even let Grey get a word in.

"You were supposed to meet your aunt on the mainland at nine o'clock for a dentist appointment! I had no idea where you were, and now she's wasted her morning and so have I."

As she took the scolding, Grey's eyes darkened. She was angry. I hoped that'd work in my favor.

"Fine," she snapped. "Let's go. I had no idea that I had a stupid dentist appointment. And don't even ask me what I was doing here!"

"I'm not interested in what you were doing here," he responded. "I'm interested in you getting to your appointment!"

"That I didn't even know I *had*!"

Grey stomped off down the trail, Ranger Johnson following.

Chris and I turned to each other. I'd been holding my breath, and I exhaled in a big rush.

"That was close," he said.

"Too close," I agreed.

"Did you notice anything wrong with him?" Chris began. "'Cause he seemed totally whacked. Am I right?" He waited for me to nod. "My mom gets really stressed out when she has a big project for work, and sometimes that makes her a little loopy and she yells at my brother and me for stupid stuff like putting the fork on the wrong side of the plate when we set the table, and that's what he reminded me of, only way worse."

"Yeah. Totally." I stared at the spot where Grey and Ranger Johnson had been, turning their exchange over and over in my head. I realized something: If he had been back to Gallops, he'd have known I was lying about my arm. And he'd have been angry instead of jittery and stressed. So something must have happened between when he left the campsite last night and came back this morning.

But Grey hadn't told him about the diamonds. And now we had them, but something still wasn't right. And maybe it was nothing, but maybe it wasn't. It definitely meant that we had to take down that sign.

"We've gotta get a phone," I said. "And a boat."

21

"We'll go home if we get caught. And maybe bounced out of the troop," I said. Chris and I were working out our plan. Taking a boat—okay, stealing a boat—and going over to the other islands, after we'd been expressly forbidden to, broke about 3,230 rules involving safety, scout behavior, and, to get technical—the law.

"Yeah," said Chris, "but if he thinks you're hiding what really happened with your arm—and you definitely hurt it on Gallops—he's going to want to figure out what we were doing. And who knows how long Grey will stay mad at him and not mention the diamonds?"

I hoped so. "I'm not sure what's going on with him, but yeah, we have to have the story about my arm match. Plus, Derek knows that we're looking for the diamonds too. Even though he doesn't know we have them, Ranger Johnson could maybe have him check our tent or something." I took a breath. Something else had occurred to me. "We might also want to move the rest of the diamonds, in case Grey tells him about the cave."

Chris nodded. He reached into the pocket of his shorts and brought out the mints tin.

"What about these?"

"We hide 'em," I replied. I rubbed my eyes. I'd never been this tired before in my life. Plus, today there was no breeze to take the edge off the sticky heat. We may as well have been in the middle of a parking lot instead of on an island, the way the sun baked us. I swatted a fly.

"Let's go back. I gotta go down to the dock and take a better look at how the boats are stored." Chris handed the diamonds to me and I dropped them in my shorts pocket. I buttoned the flap.

On our way down to the campsite, voices came from up ahead of us. We slowed down.

Pete. And Derek.

A burst of adrenaline went through me. I tugged Chris off the path and behind a low wall. The guys were talking about the firecrackers the night before, laughing over how scared everyone had been.

"Did you see his face?" Derek mimicked Ranger Johnson's wild eyes and open mouth when we raced out of our tents. "Priceless."

Pete laughed and did his own impersonation. They were so into their reenactment that a herd of elephants could have snuck up on them.

I got my kill sticker ready, and Chris and I split up. He cut around so he'd be in front of them, I stayed behind.

"Hey, have you guys seen a blue Sox hat anywhere?" Chris called. "It fell off my pack and I've been looking for it everywhere. Derek? You seen it? Hey Pete, how's the poison ivy healing? I had that last summer wicked bad on my legs . . ." He just kept motoring along, walking toward them. Derek and Pete watched, waiting to get a word in, backs to me.

I crept down the path in a low crouch, sticker pinched between my fingers, arm extended, heart pounding. When I was less than ten feet away, I sprang forward.

"Gotcha!" I cried, and stabbed it right between Pete's shoulder blades. He stumbled forward, almost taking Chris out. I nearly fell too, but windmilled my arms and kept my balance.

"You little—" Derek lunged for Chris, who backpedaled out of his reach.

"Fair and square, D," Chris jeered. We high-fived. "You guys need to be more alert."

Pete twisted his torso one way and then the other, trying to get a look at the sticker that was firmly planted on his back.

Derek's face flushed an ugly brick color. "You little rats. You think you're so smart." You'd think it was him who'd been tagged.

Pete shrugged. "Dude, he got me. It's part of the game." He fished around in his pocket and handed me a slip of paper with my next kill's name on it: Manuel Ramierez.

Manny.

Crap.

Chris and I relived the kill on the way back to camp. Pete and Derek had stayed behind, Derek probably plotting a way to take me out.

"So who'd you get next?" Chris asked.

"Uh, I didn't even look," I lied. I pretended to fish through my pockets. We were getting closer to camp, and I hoped I could stall him. Having Manny could give me an easy out—just never tag him, let Cam tag me, and Cam could deal with Manny.

But tagging someone was fun. My head buzzed and my heart was still beating fast. I *liked* it.

My fingers brushed against the cool tin of diamonds. Jeepers, these pockets had some secrets.

Mr. Fuentes spotted us. "Boys!" He waved us over. Grateful for the distraction, I brought my hands out of my pockets and we headed over to meet him.

"I need you to do me a favor. We have a pile of paperwork for the scouts applying for merit badges this trip. Doug was supposed to organize it today, so we could see who has outstanding requirements before the end of camp. But, as you know, he's not here. Can you handle it?"

"Sure," Chris said. He took the papers from Mr. Fuentes, who handed me a clipboard and pencil. We sat in the shadow of one of the tents, and with Chris reading off the names and completed requirements, and me marking them down, we finished them just before lunch.

"Where's Jack?" Chris asked a half hour later. He was plowing through his third pb&j sandwich, with two more stacked on his plate. It took a lot of food to keep that engine going.

"Haven't seen him since we finished our census this morning," Manny said. He chugged from his water bottle and wiped his mouth with the back of his hand. "That was a few hours ago."

Chris, Manny, and I exchanged glances, then looked around the campsite. Every other scout was there, eating lunch. As though he read our minds, Mr. Fuentes called out, "Where's Jack? Anybody seen him?"

The group was silent. "I'll check the tent," said Manny, "in case he's asleep or somethin'."

He navigated through the crowd of guys around the fire pit and headed toward our tent. I knew Manny wouldn't find him. Immediately, I looked at Steve, who wore a tight smirk.

"Revenge," I said to Chris.

"Yeah." He sighed. "This isn't going to be pretty." He stuck one of the sandwiches in his pocket, the other he tore into three large pieces and stuffed them into his mouth, one at a time.

Manny came back—no Jack.

Mr. Fuentes directed us to break into teams and search the island.

"He can't have gone far," he said. "He's probably taking a nap somewhere. Happens every year."

He wasn't napping. Chris, Manny, and I decided to take the beach.

"Last year," Chris said as we walked, "one of the guys—he was a senior—found a kid napping and poured honey on his sneakers. That's why we don't have it at breakfast anymore."

"What's that do?" asked Manny. "You can wash that off."

"Yeah, after you get the million ants off them," Chris said. He shuddered. "The kid had nightmares so bad, he had to go home."

I couldn't blame him.

We came out to the beach. No Jack.

"Should we walk down a little bit?" Manny asked. "He could be on the far end."

We headed in that direction, occasionally calling Jack, and after we'd been walking for a couple of minutes, we heard him yell.

"Hey, guys! Over here!"

The three of us turned in all directions. "Where in the—" said Manny.

"Oh. Crap," said Chris. "Found him." He pointed toward the trees.

There, in the shade, crouched low to the ground, was Jack. Just Jack. No clothes. No shoes. Nothin' but his bright white self.

"What the hell?" Chris said. He stripped off his outer long-sleeved Cape Cod T-shirt and tossed it to Jack, who looked simultaneously grateful and like he didn't know what to do with it.

"Tie it around your waist," I suggested.

He tied it with the shirt hanging in front, sleeves in back. The sight cracked us up.

"What happened?" Manny finally asked.

"I went for a walk this morning," he said, "and I got really hot. There was no one around, and I didn't have my trunks, so . . ." We nodded. Bad choice, but whatever.

"So I guess Steve and Derek had been following me. I tossed my stuff on the beach, and they picked it up. I didn't want to walk back to the campsite because, uh, I didn't want to get a . . . sunburn. I'm glad you guys came along. You didn't bring any sunscreen, did you?" he asked hopefully.

"Sorry," I answered. "No sunscreen."

"We've still gotta walk back," Manny pointed out. "And unless you plan on using that shirt as an umbrella, something's going to get pink."

"Oh, well." Jack shrugged. We picked our way across the beach and to the path to the campsite. "Steve's face was totally worth it."

Back at the tent, Jack covered up and Chris told me he was going to the tide pool walk. We still hadn't looked at the boats, and we'd head back to Gallops tonight to take down the sign. I hoped it wasn't too late. I decided to go with him. It'd be a good opportunity to see if Ranger Johnson's demeanor changed from this morning.

We got to the meeting spot a couple of minutes early. The tide was almost completely out, and Lovells became a completely different island. Acres and acres of rocky sea floor were exposed, revealing small tide pools and habitats for all kinds of tiny sea creatures. Normally I'd be into seeing what was left behind by the sea, but today all I could think about was our impending adventure.

Sneaking out was best left to Moxie. She was really good at it; I was much more of a rule-follower.

Or I had been, anyway. Maybe that was something else that had changed over this summer. I didn't even want to think of the number of rules I'd be breaking tonight. But doing something for the right reasons evened it out. I hoped.

Cam, Steve, and Ravi arrived before Ranger Johnson. The other guys tossed rocks at the waves and cracked up about Steve's revenge on Jack. Chris and I checked out the rowboats, which had been dragged far beyond the high tide line, at the top of one of the dunes.

"Score!" Chris said. They weren't tied up or anything.

"But look," I said, pointing out to sea. The small Sunfishes were obviously hooked to one another, and a buoy. "I bet they're locked somehow."

"Not necessarily," Chris said. "They don't have to be, if you take the oars from the rowboats. No way to get to them."

"No way for us to get to them either," I pointed out.

"Oh, but if I volunteer to do check-down here tonight, there is," he replied. Each night before dinner, scouts had to sign up to check specific areas of the camp to make sure everything was put away or set up properly for the next day. I'd mostly stuck to site-specific checks, like checking the compasses and other orienteering equipment.

"Perfect," I said, and swallowed. Even though I was nervous, I couldn't deny the thrill that I felt knowing we were really going to do this.

After all that, Ranger Johnson still hadn't shown up.

"Dude, this is lame," Steve said. He twisted one of his dread-locks. "I'm going back to the site to take a nap. This guy isn't coming." He and his buddies left Chris and me alone on the beach. The ranger was at least a half hour late.

"Do we take off?"

I shrugged. "Sure. I don't think he's coming. Something happened this morning, obviously." I just hoped he hadn't gone to Gallops to check out my story.

We watched the water for a minute, pulling farther and farther away from us, then turned to go.

Ranger Johnson was about ten feet behind us.

"Sorry I'm late," he said.

If it was possible, he looked worse than he had in the morning. His shirt showed damp sweat rings under each arm, and his right eyelid twitched.

"Are you okay, Ranger?" Chris started. "You really don't look good. Maybe you should lie down or something? Are you feeling sick? Seasick? Do you even get seasick?"

I let Chris go while I watched Ranger Johnson. He quite obviously wasn't paying attention to Chris's words. His eyes were focused on some point out to sea, and he nibbled on a cuticle.

"No," he said. "Not really." He paused. "I need you to think very, very carefully, boys. Have you found anything—*anything*—that could be Long Ben Avery's treasure? It's very important that you tell me the truth now."

Chris and I exchanged looks. I don't know what Chris was thinking, but this was not the behavior of a guy who wanted to put treasure in a museum. If I had had any doubts about withholding info from the ranger, they were gone.

"No sir," I responded. "Unfortunately not." Did he know I was lying?

"Have you seen Derek?"

"No. But he's probably in some other afternoon session," I added, hoping Ranger Johnson would say more.

Instead of speaking, he shook his head.

"Okay. Go look for hermit crabs," he said, and started walking, head down, watching just a few feet in front of him.

"There's one!" Chris cried. He pointed. The little guy, spindly legs tap dancing on the rocks, scuttled into a crevice.

"Great," Ranger Johnson said. "Okay, boys. You keep looking. I have to, uh, go now."

We stared at him, incredulous. He wiped his face with his hands, and, not making eye contact, turned and walked away, back toward the road—and camp.

"You thinking what I'm thinking?" Chris said.

"Oh, yeah. We're following him."

22

We stayed silent, several yards behind Ranger Johnson. But much like Derek and Poison Ivy Pete earlier, he wouldn't have heard us if we were the entire Chestnut College marching band.

He walked, but only barely—his speed was just shy of a run. I had to hustle to keep up with him, and in the still air, soon I had sweat rings on my T-shirt too. He kept fidgeting, even when he was walking: His fingers were always in his hair, or plucking at something on his shirt, or in his mouth. The guy was a total wreck.

When we neared our campsite, he slowed down, and so did we. A couple of scouts sat in the shade on the edge of the site, and he asked them if they'd seen Derek. They pointed across the site, but we couldn't hear what they said.

"What does he want with DB?" Chris whispered.

"Diamonds," I reminded him.

"Oh yeah."

We spotted Derek at the same time Ranger Johnson did: He was working on a merit badge with a group at one of the battlements, back to us.

Chris and I skirted the group and went down to the lower

side of the battlement, so we couldn't see anything, but we could hear them.

Ranger Johnson cleared his throat. "Derek. May I see you for a moment?"

Derek grunted. They walked to the next battlement; Chris and I pressed ourselves against the wall, which was warm from the sun.

"What have you found?" Ranger Johnson asked. His voice sounded a little crackly, like it hadn't changed yet. More nerves?

"Nothing," Derek said. "Those spots were a total bust, right? And now we're stuck here. I can't even look for you."

"You must've found *something*," Ranger Johnson continued. "I know the treasure is there."

There was silence for a second.

"Um, no." Derek said. "Look, it's a story. The treasure has been missing for hundreds of years. I think it's great that you want to put it in a museum somewhere, but a bunch of scouts aren't going to be the ones to find it. You probably need—I dunno—equipment or something. A metal detector, maybe? You'd know more about that than I do."

Ranger Johnson barked a short laugh. "Oh, you'd think that," he said. "You'd think that. But no, I don't really know anything about it. But I need to. Do you know anything else? Anything at all?"

I raised an eyebrow at Chris. This was freaky. It was a total change from the accusing Ranger Johnson that I'd seen the other day, but this version—pleading, whining Ranger Johnson— seemed even more dangerous: Like a dog that was hurt and could attack at any second. Even though there were kids just a few feet away, all of a sudden I was nervous for Derek.

"No, dude. I don't. It's just a story anyway. I mean, I'm sure the treasure is buried somewhere—isn't that what pirates *did?*— but I have no idea where. Someone probably found it eons ago."

"Um, I really need to get back to my group, so . . ." He trailed off. Ranger Johnson didn't make a sound. "So . . . um, are we good here?"

Still no response.

"Okay, then. I'm just gonna go back . . ." A crunch of leaves, and Derek left. Ranger Johnson, as far as we could tell, hadn't moved.

Chris motioned for us to leave, and we crept away from the battlement, around the fort, to the road. He opened his mouth, and I held up one finger to wait. We needed to put some distance between us and the ranger.

A few yards later, I stopped and stepped off the path. Chris followed.

"Crazy," was the first word out of his mouth.

"Totally," I agreed. "We have to get to that island tonight and move those diamonds. I don't even care what the consequences are."

DAY 10

CHRIS'S GOTCHA! ALIVE/TAGGED LIST

STEVE

D-BAG DEREK

~~ME (CHRIS)~~

JACK

MANNY

~~DOUG~~ (left camp)

~~PETE~~

~~HORATIO~~

CAM

~~JORGE~~

RAVI

OLLIE

23

We had to wait until Manny came back from his swim to commit grand-theft boat, as we were pretty sure he was the last person awake in camp. Chris and I debated bringing Jack and Manny into our plan, but the less they knew about this outing, the better.

It was a struggle to stay awake. I recited the alphabet backward, pictured every cache I'd hidden in our junior high, and even picked at my healing scabs to avoid closing my eyes.

Finally, Manny slipped back into the tent and into his sleeping bag. According to what the guys told me, I was supposed to take myself out instead of him. Could I do it? I didn't know.

He settled down and his breathing gradually slowed. When the snores started, I sat up. Chris was across from me, wide-awake, whispering to himself.

"Ready?"

He nodded.

Both of us were dressed in T-shirts and swim trunks. We slipped out of the sleeping bags and out the back flap of the tent. I'd stashed my backpack in the brush just beyond the campsite, and I retrieved it while Chris scanned the camp to see if anyone else was up. Dr. Gupta hadn't come back from bringing Doug to

Boston, leaving just Mr. Fuentes with us. Ranger Johnson, who I thought was supposed to stay at the campsite, didn't show. Grey's mom was in Milwaukee, so maybe he had to stay at home with her? Or maybe she had gone to Boston after all?

We made our way down the main path to the beach, not saying a word. The moon was almost full, casting a blue light on the plants and path. The salty-stingy smell of the ocean seemed stronger at night, or maybe I'd just stopped noticing it during the day?

We reached the beach. Waves licked the rocky shore. The tide was coming in, fingers of water stretching toward the beached boats.

"I put them over here," Chris said, and he headed to a clump of trees where the sand met the brush. I dropped my backpack at one of the rowboats and followed him.

Until we got the oars, I wasn't worried. Kids like Manny snuck around the island all the time at night. We'd get in trouble if we were caught, but not the same type of trouble we'd get in if we left the island.

And we were going to leave the island.

We dropped the oars next to one of the rowboats.

"Are you sure this is a good idea?" Chris asked, whispering.

"No," I replied honestly. "But I don't know what else we *can* do, if we want to keep the diamonds safe. Do you really want to hand them over to Ranger Johnson?"

He shook his head. "Dude, no way." We put the oars and my backpack in the bottom of the boat, then Chris and I slid it over the rocks toward the water. I was sure that the grating, grinding sound of wood on rock would wake everyone from Cape Cod to Marblehead, but no searchlights came from the sky, no voices shouted at us to stop. And once we were in up to our knees, the sound disappeared and it was only the water lapping at the wood. We guided the boat out 'til the ocean was up to our waists. I flopped in first, then Chris.

He passed me an oar.

A cold fear hugged my heart, and the sensation was worse than any asthma attack. This was real. And more than any escapade in downtown Boston at night, this was dangerous. We were on the ocean. *In the dark. In a boat!*

I swallowed the fear as best I could. The diamonds were somehow important. We had to move them, keep them safe 'til we could call Agent Goh and let him know where they were. I kept telling myself that, repeating it like a mantra, until my heart slowed down.

Plus, the rhythm of rowing helped me relax. The Sunfishes weren't that far off shore. We thunk-splashed the rowboat through waves that glinted with moonlight. Chris switched the lines with precision, and I clambered from one boat to another.

Chris directed me on what lines to hold or untie, and soon we were gliding toward Gallops. The wind was light, but the sail filled and pushed us right along. I even ducked when Chris said "Boom!"

"I can't believe we did this, man," said Chris.

"Tell me about it," I said. "We're not back yet, though."

In a few minutes, we were nearing the beach. Chris pulled the rudder up and hopped in the water up to his armpits to guide us in. I got out too, flopping in and making a bigger splash than I'd intended.

We dragged the boat up high on shore. The island was silent and dark. No one was allowed to camp here, so we would be totally alone.

"Now what?" Chris asked.

Truthfully, I hadn't thought that far ahead.

We stood on the beach, the waves swooshing across the shore and a jet roaring in for a landing at Logan across the harbor. Sounds carry so much farther at night.

"We want to get the diamonds from the cave and find a new hiding place," I said, thinking the steps through and feeling more confident. "So let's go back there first." I pulled my GPS out of my backpack and punched in the coordinates. The little compass started blinking, and we followed the arrow.

Chris yawned and I caught it. I had no idea what time it was. Two a.m.? Three? How much time did we have before the boats started coming through the harbor? Or what if Manny or Jack woke up and freaked out that we were gone? There were so many ways we could get caught. I tried not to think of the what-ifs and just follow the path around the island.

Our eyes were well adjusted to the dark, but it was still hard to pick our way over the cracked pavement. Chris and I stayed silent, eyes on the ground.

One creepy thing about being out on Gallops at night? All the rabbits. We'd seen a ton during the day, but now, their favorite time to be out, they were *everywhere*. You don't think of rabbits as sinister animals, but their constant munching on the grass sounded ominous.

"Here," whispered Chris. He was right. We were at the spot where we'd been fixing the retaining wall when Grey came with the water bottle. How angry would she be that we were doing this without her—for a second time?

Furious, probably.

We passed the building foundation and slid down the hill to the beach. The GPS was blinking steadily as if I didn't know we were here.

In front of us was the berm. In the dark, you couldn't tell that anyone had been in there. During the day, maybe we'd see disturbed sand and broken branches, but now? No way.

I clipped a small light to the front of my Sox cap and hitched my backpack onto both shoulders.

"Let's go," I said, and clicked the light on.

Getting into the cave was easier this time—third time's a charm, right?—and I rolled to the side to give Chris a space to land.

A couple of seconds later we were crowded in front of the hole in the wall where my arm had discovered a three-centuries-old secret. And it didn't occur to me until right then that Grey might have moved the "rocks" herself. I crossed my fingers and sent up a wish.

The yellow circle of light from my cap revealed the rough rectangle with splintered, jagged edges. Chris hissed between his teeth, looking at them.

"I know, right?" I whispered.

Gingerly, I extended my good arm and threaded through the needles of wood. I cringed, expecting my fingers to get bitten off or land in something gross—guess I have a fear of sticking my arm in places that I can't see into—but all I felt were cold, hard rocks.

Diamonds.

I fished around, grabbing as many as I could, and pulled out my hand—giving myself a new scratch.

"Gotcha," Chris breathed. I opened my palm: eight rocks, looking just as dirty and grungy as the initial ones we'd found.

"There are more in there." I closed my fist and rubbed at the fresh scratch. "We're going to look like porcupines when we're done."

I pulled a pillowcase out of my bag. Back at camp, I'd been stuffing it with my sweatshirt to sleep on, but it had a better job now. The diamonds clicked as they fell against one another.

"Try this." Chris took one of his shirts off, shook it out, and folded it into a thick rectangle. Then he draped it over the edge of the hole. At least we wouldn't get as many scratches.

"Nice. Go ahead," I offered. "Grab some."

Chris's eyes glittered in the dark, and he stuck his hand in and came out with another fistful. All in all, we dumped about six handfuls each into the pillowcase. It weighed as much as my laptop.

"There's a lot of stuff in there," he said. We peered into the sack, which was filthy. "Oh, crud!" he added as I tied it off.

"What?" I thought he saw a light or heard someone.

"Did you bring the box?"

I shook my head. "We can't leave those in here," I explained. "We need to have ones to show the FBI, to prove we're telling the truth." Chris stuck the rocks into my backpack and zipped it up. I was carrying pirate treasure! This was almost the weirdest thing that had ever happened to me.

"Are we taking them back with us?" Chris asked.

"We can't," I said. "There are too many people at camp. What if the ranger sends Derek to snoop in our tent? Or what if one of the other guys finds them? It's too risky."

"We could just *tell* the other guys," Chris said. "The more people that know, the better, right?"

"Not really. People flip out," I said. "There's always someone who wants to talk you out of doing what's right, into doing what they want. Seriously, I trust Agent Goh. He'll do what's right for the treasure. Let's hide them here, and we can tell the FBI where to find them."

We climbed out of the cave and I clicked off my light. I expected the sky to be bleeding dawn, but it was still pitch dark. The moon had moved. I'd lost all sense of time—not urgency, though.

We had to find a new hiding spot.

Chris and I stood on one of the broken paths around the base of a building. We'd walked inland, scouting for hiding places, but so much of the island had been developed at one time—and the rabbits had feasted on so many plants and small trees—that the landscape was awkward for hiding anything.

A blue-and-white pillowcase, especially. We'd decided that the asbestos-filled buildings were probably our best bet, since people had to stay away from them.

"What does asbestos do to you?" Chris asked.

"Dunno," I said. "I don't think I'd even know it if I saw it."

He pulled his now-grungy T-shirt up over his nose and mouth.

We peeked over the wall of one of the foundations into a deep basement pit. Metal rods poked out from the crumbling walls, and loose rocks, leaves, and debris cluttered ledges and stairs.

We couldn't see the bottom.

"This is the place," I said. "Even if someone spots the pillow-case, they'll think it's garbage."

There was a spot at the edge of the foundation where the wall was a little lower, near a staircase. I heaved myself up and Chris came beside me. We balanced along the wall to the stairs, gravel kicking out from under our feet and clattering down into the pit. I gulped.

"Don't slip," Chris said, his voice muffled.

We reached the staircase and carefully climbed down, testing our weight on the stone steps. They held. There was no railing, just steep, leaf-slick stairs to the bottom. A few times I felt my waterlogged sneakers sliding out from under me, but I managed to keep my balance.

Until the second-to-last one.

My left foot came down on a thick, spongy patch of leaves—and kept going forward. I tipped backward, pinwheeling my arms and grabbing at the wall, which didn't help. My butt and lower back slammed into the hard stone, and I bumped down the rest of the way, landing in a pile of muck, left leg painfully twisting under me.

"Ollie! You okay?" Chris gave me a hand.

"Yeah," I said, shaky from the fall. I tried to brush the goop off me, but it just disintegrated or smeared across my legs and swim trunks. I tried not to imagine how much rabbit poop was mixed in with the leaves. My back and leg throbbed. I was going to have an awesome bruise.

Luckily, my clip-light had stayed attached to my hat. I turned it on.

The space was huge—nearly as big as my school's auditorium—but it wasn't perfectly square. Several inches of muck littered the floor, along with garbage. I spotted a few plastic bags, a faded Dunkin' Donuts cup, and a bright green plastic plate.

We walked around for a few minutes, looking at the site. Even with the light, it was tough to see well, and I felt like I wasn't doing a good enough job assessing hiding spots. But we didn't have time. And now I was not only exhausted, but hurt.

"Here," I said. There was a piece of the wall that jutted out, with a lot of loose rocks at the bottom. I tugged the pillowcase of diamonds out of my bag, then Chris and I moved the pile of rocks, nestling the pillowcase in the middle. We put some stones and leaves on top of it, and voila! The perfect hiding place.

Chris paused. "I can't believe it," he whispered. "Ollie, do you know how much this is going to change our lives?"

My heart kind of ached when he said that. *Thinking* about those changes is a lot different than actually living through those changes. But what could I tell him? That he'd find himself not trusting people? Hiding from the news? Not really sure who he was?

"You can only imagine," is what I said. He turned to leave.

"Wait!" I said. I grabbed the GPS. Even though I could barely see the screen, I knew the button combination to "save location" by heart. I marked the spot. Once that was done, I followed Chris up the stairs—slowly—and to the wall. My back twinged with every step.

Once we were on the path back to the beach, I felt lighter. Even if Grey told Ranger Johnson about the cave, there'd be no way he could find the diamonds before we got off the island and called the authorities. Chris—and Grey, if she wanted it— could have their moment of glory, and even with the weird way the ranger had been acting, he'd be psyched that his daughter found treasure. Maybe he'd even be impressed with what she'd done instead of worried about where she was.

When we came out to the beach, though, any relief I'd been feeling drifted away. The sky had changed from black to dark blue, and straight out to the east, the water was starting to glow. We'd been out all night, and still had to get back.

We hurried to where we'd left the Sunfish. I tossed my backpack in, and we slid it down the gravelly beach to the sea, not caring how much noise we made.

It was only when we were sailing back, several hundred yards from shore, that I remembered:

I'd left the No Trespassing sign still standing.

24

There wasn't anything I could do about it, but I still stressed as we crossed between the islands. Chris guided the Sunfish up to the float, and I unclipped the line from the rowboat and onto the sailboat, yawning as I did so. I turned to Chris, who was bringing down the sail, and caught a wide-eyed expression on his face.

"Grab the boat!" he cried.

Huh?

"The boat!"

I looked from side to side. What was he . . . ?

Crud. The rowboat. It had floated out of its parking spot and was headed out to open water.

"Get it!"

It was too far away for me to reach. I groaned, but kicked off my sneakers and jumped into the harbor, the chill in the water pushing away any sleep fog in my brain. There was no way for me to hang on to the boat, so I had to sort of nudge it with my shoulder while I paddled closer to the sailboat. Chris grabbed the side so it wouldn't float away again.

Now I had to heave myself up and over, into the rowboat. I gripped the edge, but pulling my body into the rowboat from deep water was way harder than flopping in when the water was up to my waist. My arms shook with the effort, and the whole boat listed toward me. I kind of threw myself in, kicking with my legs, and smacked my cheek on one of the benches.

"You nearly pulled my arm out of the socket!"

"Sorry. I'm not a skilled maritime expert," I replied, wincing as I pressed on my cheekbone. I could add another bruise to the night's collection.

"Hold the boat." I hung on to the Sunfish and took inventory of my aches and pains while Chris finished wrapping and tying lines: back (from the fall), shoulders (from rowing), cheek. I shivered in the light breeze.

Chris slipped into the rowboat like an eel and handed me an oar. Back throbbing with each stroke, we headed to shore.

"Take your oars out," Chris whispered once we got close enough to clearly see the beach. "The waves will carry us in."

We bobbed along. I kept my eyes on the beach, trying to ignore the pink-and-golden-streaked sky behind me.

A few waves later, Chris decided that we were close enough to the beach to hop out and walk the boat in. You'd think that being in the water three times already would have me prepared for the cold, but nope. I still gasped—which sent me into a coughing fit. Doubled over, I hung on to the edge of the rowboat. It rocked as Chris came out behind me.

When I caught my breath and straightened, I scanned the beach again. Empty. We walked the boat in, waves gently nudging us toward shore. I kept my eyes at the water in front of me. The beach was rocky, and sharp shells easily slice open a foot.

Not that looking ahead would've helped.

The bottom of the rowboat scraped shore, and as we switched from guiding to sliding, a low whistle came from the beach in front of us.

"Enjoy your seaside adventure, guys?"

Derek.

I wanted to throw up. Seriously, I'd have preferred that Mr. Fuentes had been on the beach. What the heck was Derek doing up so early, anyway?

"I watched you the whole way," he said. Chris and I stood ankle deep in water, the rowboat between us. There was nothing we could do or say.

Derek smirked. "You two are so dead. You'll be banned from Wilderness Scouts for *life* when Mr. Fuentes finds out. You went back to Gallops, didn't you? Thinking you'd find some buried treasure? How *lame*."

I glanced at Chris. His lips were clamped tightly together, like they were a dam holding back a flood. Which they kinda were.

I took a breath. "We were exploring," I said, trying to sound casual over my hammering heart. "Everyone in my troop does it."

Derek snorted and crossed his arms. "Yeah, right. Sneaking off the island? That's not exploring, that's suicide."

"*We* made it back." I shrugged. "So have the guys in my troop. Gotcha! game doesn't quite compare."

Derek's eyes narrowed at the insult. "Well, it doesn't fly here.

Mr. Fuentes is going to have you on a boat by lunchtime, Doc."

"Sure, if you're a snitch. We've gotta beach the boat." I hoped I hadn't gone too far. "Let's go," I directed at Chris.

We heaved the boat, and Derek waited for a second, then stepped aside. His breath blew hot on my neck as I struggled the boat past him.

"Nice eye. Run into any pirates?" he asked. I ignored him.

We slid the boat next to its mate, then Chris put the oars back where he'd left them yesterday afternoon. Derek stood to the side, watching us the whole time but not offering a hand to help. My limbs felt like granite, my back screamed, and my cheek throbbed from where I hit it on the boat. I slipped into my sneakers. All I wanted was a comfy bed and about sixteen hours of sleep.

The sun was completely over the horizon. It had to be just before seven. The rest of camp would be up soon, if they weren't already.

Chris and I started to cross the beach to the path back to camp, but Derek stopped us.

"I win Gotcha! no one knows about your little excursion." I considered the offer. There was no way for me to guarantee his win. I could be taken out; plenty of guys were still in the game—including Manny. And someone had Derek.

"There's no way for Ollie to make sure that you win," Chris said, unable to keep quiet any longer. Words poured from him like the waves tumbling on shore. "Even if he said yes, he could get out tomorrow and then it wouldn't matter. So that's a lame way to blackmail someone." He clamped his mouth shut.

Derek ignored him, just leveled his eyes at me. And it took me a second, but I got it: I had to finish the game. It had to come down to me and Derek.

And then I'd have to lose. And lose big. I considered it.

"Gotcha," I muttered.

25

When Chris and I got back to camp, everyone was up. We claimed that we went for an early-morning swim and that I'd banged into one of the pilings under the dock and bruised my cheek. I'm not sure Mr. F. bought it, but he didn't press me on it. After breakfast my eyes were so heavy I could barely focus on Mr. Fuentes's wilderness survival lecture.

Neither could he, evidently. Ranger Johnson was supposed to show up and give it, and he was nowhere to be found.

Call it an "educated guess": I was pretty sure I knew where he was.

Anyway, by the time lunch was over, I was dead. So I staked out a spot, pulled my hat over my eyes, and hoped that the rabbits, Wilderness Scouts, and other animals would leave me alone. I didn't even care if someone tagged me, I was that tired.

The heat and exhaustion combined to send me into a deep, black sleep. The kind of sleep where you don't dream, just collapse into nothingness.

Until someone sticks something cold on your leg.

I yelled and sat up straight. Completely disoriented, I flailed around for my clock radio—which was approximately fifteen miles west, as the crow flies. My asthma kicked in and my chest locked up tighter than a bank vault.

"Ollie! Ollie! Jeez! Calm down! Breathe!"

Grey.

I wasn't at home. I was on an island.

I caught her wide eyes and mouth in a big O, then the only thing I paid attention to was my pocket. I fumbled and pulled out my inhaler. My heart jammed in my chest, and I held the medicinal cloud in as long as I could. My airways relaxed, and I coughed—which made my back hurt.

Oh *yeah*, I was on an island.

"You okay?" she asked. "I didn't mean to send you into shock, but we need to talk."

I shook my head, embarrassed. "I'm okay." I coughed again. "Just . . . surprised."

She handed me an icy can of Coke—contraband. No soda allowed in Wilderness Scout camp. I cracked the tab and took a big gulp. A different relief flowed through me.

While I sipped, she sat next to me, braiding her ponytail.

"So," she said finally, twisting a tie-thing around the end of her hair. "Uh, you know how my dad's been acting a little weird, right?"

I nodded, thrown off. I thought she wanted to talk about the diamonds.

"Yeah. He's been really freaked. So I called him out on it last night. My mom's away, and I . . . ya know, wanted to know what the deal was. I thought maybe they're getting divorced or she left or something—she hates living out here, is always complaining about how lonely it is and how there's nothing to do. She's not like my dad and me. I could stay out here forever." She fiddled with the end of her braid.

I didn't know what to say to this softer version of Grey. "Are they . . . okay?" I tried.

She nodded. "Yeah. That's what he *said*, anyway. He promised, actually. But there's something else up. I mean—obviously. You saw him yesterday."

"Yeah."

"But it was weird. You know how he made a big deal about that dentist appointment, and my aunt waiting for me? I totally didn't have one. It's next week. He had the day all wrong. It's like he wants me off the island. He spent all night studying these old maritime maps, looking for more treasure sites."

A sick feeling crawled through my stomach.

"Did he ask about the diamonds?" I said.

"He did," Grey said. "I didn't tell him anything. I mean, I wanted to, but he seemed so weird about it, you know?"

"Yeah," I said slowly. Was she telling me the truth? How would I know?

"Maybe we should just tell him," Grey said. A worried line creased her forehead. "Something is definitely wrong here."

"Maybe that's why we shouldn't tell him," I tried. "I mean, if you don't know what the deal is . . ."

"He's my *dad*, Ollie, not some criminal!"

She was right, but my gut was telling me that telling Ranger Johnson we had the diamonds was the exact *wrong* thing to do. I couldn't say anything bad about him. But . . .

"We made a deal, and Chris was in on it. We should at least ask him how he feels before you do anything," I tried. And hoped . . .

She dropped the end of her braid and sighed. "Okay. Fine. We'll let him vote too. But no matter what Chris says, I think we need to tell my dad about the rocks. Maybe we should count them too, to know how many there are."

Counting the rocks was a good idea. I wished we had thought of it. This was not good. She was going to be mad.

"Well, that's a great idea," I began, choosing my words carefully. "But . . . um, things kind of changed last night. Chris and I were talking, and we thought we should probably change their hiding place."

Grey nodded. "Totally. I was thinking we could put them in this huge hollow oak tree, on the north side of the island. There's an old bee's nest in it—no one would spot it." She knew everything about these islands. Maybe I should've talked to her before we moved the diamonds . . .

Too late.

"Uh, well." I straightened up more and crossed my legs. "See, the thing is, Chris and I were worried that someone would find the hole in the cave wall. Really worried. So, we, uh . . ." Her expression was open, curious, but the longer I spoke, the darker it became.

"You moved them already." Voice flat, eyes hard.

I gulped. "Last night. We snuck over after midnight. We wanted you to come, but . . ."

"But *nothing*," she snapped. "I showed you where the cave *was*! Bad enough you went back there *once* without me. And you just told me we had to have *all three of us* vote before we told my dad we had the diamonds! And you went behind my back and did *this*? You guys suck." She got up and stomped off. "Enjoy your Coke, *traitor*!" she called out.

She was right. We did suck.

I tried to tell myself that we'd done the right thing. Something *was* going on with her dad. But it didn't make me feel better.

I swigged the Coke, which tasted sticky and too sweet—like deceit.

DAY 11

CHRIS'S GOTCHA! ALIVE/TAGGED LIST

STEVE

D-BAG DEREK

~~ME (CHRIS)~~

JACK

MANNY

~~DOUG~~ (left camp)

~~PETE~~

~~HORATIO~~

CAM

~~JORGE~~

RAVI

OLLIE

26

Midnight.

You'd think I'd be asleep—heck, I *wanted* to be sleeping—but I had to stay awake until Manny left for his swim. Ten nights in a row and man, was he proud of his streak. Chris's and Jack's breathing had slowed, and Manny slipped out of his sleeping bag, trunks and T-shirt on, and went out through the tent flap.

I followed him.

Along with the exhaustion pounding behind my eyes, and sore muscles from the Gallops Island exploits, my stomach had started a revolution. It churned with acid from the stress, and I kept burping.

I had to tag Manny.

I didn't want to tag Manny.

I wasn't *supposed* to tag Manny. I'd be a total outcast.

I had to tag Manny.

I promised Derek it'd come down to the two of us.

I sighed and made my way down the trail to the beach. I'd let Manny splash around or whatever, then get him on the way back to the tent. I hoped he wouldn't be as ticked off at me as I thought he would. I'd be adding him to the list of People Who

Hate Ollie, currently populated with Grey and Derek.

I sat on top of the hill that overlooked the beach, in the shadow of the trees. Manny loped down to the water, tossed his T-shirt on the sand, and dove in. While he swam, I raised my eyes to the dark smudge across the harbor that was Gallops Island.

Had I done the right thing? Should I have even gotten involved with the diamonds in the first place? If I hadn't, I'd probably be down there with Manny. Or sleeping. Derek wouldn't have seen us on the beach, and I wouldn't have to tag Manny. I'd still be someone's sidekick, instead of the leader of a diamond-hiding ring.

My life was way easier when it was about caching and video games.

Manny finished his swim and headed back across the beach. I scrambled to my feet and stepped deeper into the shadows.

He was getting closer, humming under his breath—some Theo Christmas song that'd been all over the radio this summer. It drove me crazy.

He passed me, not looking around, probably thinking he was alone. It was like he was totally confident that he was getting away with sneaking out. I almost laughed, and then I kind of wished that I could be that relaxed and confident, instead of so paranoid and jumpy all the time.

I let him get a little ways ahead of me, then I crept out. Even though I was committing tent-mate betrayal, I couldn't squash the excitement that flared through me when I started after him.

The red sticker balanced on the end of my fingertip; my heart thudded. I jogged quietly to close the gap. Manny didn't even flinch when I jumped.

"Gotcha!" I shouted, and planted the sticker on his back, near his shoulder.

He turned and took a swing at me.

I ducked, but not low or fast enough, and his fist connected with the side of my head.

"Crap, Manny!"

"Ollie?" His hands were on his knees, and he shook his head in disbelief. "Seriously?"

"Sorry," I said. I coughed, feeling the bands tighten around my chest.

"C'mon, man. Really?" I could tell that Manny was shocked. He kept shaking his head, slowly. "That's low, dude. Just low. You're supposed to bow out."

I dropped my eyes to the space between us. "I know. I'm sorry. I feel really crappy about it." I cut myself off before I revealed more than I should. I couldn't tell him about Derek or the diamonds.

"Yeah. I'm sure." He glared at me. I stepped back. "My next tag is in the tent."

We walked back to the campsite in silence. He slipped under the torn flap first, not holding it for me. I went through cautiously, half expecting him to jump me on the other side.

But he didn't. When I straightened, Manny was across from me, arm extended, kill sheet in his hand. Jack was sitting up, hair in spikes, sleeping bag pooled around his waist, eyes saucer-sized. I grabbed the sheet and stuffed it in my pocket. I couldn't look at either of them.

I crawled into my sleeping bag, body aching, feeling friendless and lower than I thought possible.

No one wanted to hang out with the tent traitor. I ate breakfast alone—Chris had gone for an early swim—and no one wanted me for the morning's game of capture the flag. As Last Pick, I ended up on Steve's team—with Manny.

Great.

"You guard the flag," Steve said.

"He'll just hand it over to the other team," Manny sneered.

"Come on, Manny," I said. "It's just a game."

Manny clenched his fists. "A game you played *dirty*."

I bristled at that. "That's not true, and you know it."

"Simmer down, Benedict Arnold." Steve stepped between us. "Manny, you have flag duty instead. Ollie, you're on search."

"Fine," I grumbled. I didn't want to argue any more, but I was still ticked.

Manny shot me a dirty look. He probably didn't want to protect the flag either, but boxed himself in when he criticized me.

Right before Steve and Manny took our flag to Fort Standish, where they would be high enough to see anyone approaching from below, Steve called the team together.

"Just so we're clear on this—Gotcha! is in play," he said, staring directly at me.

I nearly groaned out loud. I was supposed to tag Steve next. I'd have to watch for Cam too.

193

We were supposed to have partners, but since I was the odd person out on our team—in more ways than one—I went off by myself. We'd strategized where the other team might have hidden their flag, and everyone seemed to think it would be in one of the gun batteries. The pairs were going to surround the batteries and try to sneak in, one at a time. I thought Derek's team would have been smarter than that, and would have put their flag on the far beach, where it would be easier to keep an eye on. I tried to tell them that, but got shot down.

"It's too far for good game play," Steve pointed out.

"That's why they're doing it," I explained. "It pulls more people from our flag."

Steve shrugged. "You can check it out, then."

The pairs of guys headed toward the gun batteries, while I turned down the path to the beach.

I had to tag Steve. It was like Derek was setting me up—which I would have believed if it weren't for the fact that Manny handed me the paper himself. For a second, I entertained the thought of just turning myself in—confessing that I'd stolen a boat and left the island. The worst that could happen was that I'd get kicked out and sent home. And really, that didn't seem so bad. Chris—and Grey, if she spoke to us again—could deal with the diamonds. The FBI would help my parents figure out what to do with me until the media moved on.

I crumpled the paper and stuffed it deep in my pocket. I couldn't let a game guide my decisions. I was going to play, get Steve, and Derek, and win—and not quit or confess or stay a sidekick forever.

Just before I got to the beach, I stepped off the path into some of the thick brush. I crouched, keeping an eye out for poison ivy, and slowly made my way to where the rocks began.

There was the flag. Wrapped around a piece of driftwood, flapping in the light breeze, its electric orange plastic-ness was hard to miss.

And the guard?

Chris.

I rocked back on my heels. Awesome. If I wanted to get the flag—and potentially restore some of my credibility with at least a few of the scouts—I'd have to outwit another tent-mate. Well, I did it once.

Hopefully Chris would take this less seriously than Manny took Gotcha!

I watched Chris for a few minutes. He fidgeted, walked toward the water, then remembered what he was supposed to be doing and came back to face the paths. I waited until he turned toward the water again, and crept out of the brush. I ran as fast as I could to the flag, sneakers skittering over the rocky beach. My fingers brushed the orange plastic.

"Hey!" Chris shouted. "Ollie!"

I tore the flag from the piece of driftwood and raced to the trees. My chest tightened with the strain and blood thumped in my ears. Behind me, Chris yelled for backup.

I had no chance of getting the flag into our territory. My stubby legs and weak lungs were not cut out for cross-country. I should've taken someone with me. I clutched the flag close to my chest, hoping that I could push a little bit farther—

Chris crashed into me like a speeding bullet; a Superman with lots and lots of padding.

I fell forward, throwing my arms out to break my fall. The flag went flying into the brush and my glasses popped off. I landed on my chest, the air whooshing out of me with a big "oof!"

"You're out!" Chris panted.

"I'm nearly dead." I took a hit from my inhaler. Would there be any medicine in there by the time I got home?

We rolled over and sat up. Chris passed me my glasses. I brushed dirt and sand off the front of my T-shirt.

"You're done," he said. "Good try, though."

I grunted and stood. Coming on my own was a stupid idea. Now I'd be out of the game completely and my team would be annoyed that I'd put Chris on guard.

That is, if they thought to check the beach before our flag was taken.

"Guess you're better at hiding stuff than retrieving it," Chris said as he fished through the thicket for the flag. "I mean, the way you hid those diamonds was pretty amazing. No one would think to look in a pillowcase—" I nudged him. Hard. Did he want everyone to know where the stuff was?

"Chris?! Seriously. Stop!"

He looked at me like I had nine heads, then his eyes got big and he understood why I was being a jerk.

We both scanned the beach. No one around.

I trudged to the water. If you were caught, you were supposed to sit in "jail," near the other team's flag. If their flag was stolen, you were free.

The waves pulled back and forth from shore. Ahead of me, across the water, was Gallops Island. Its trees and scrubby beach seemed so close. Were the diamonds safe? Had Ranger Johnson gone to look for them? Or someone else? A gull cried, then landed in the waves a short distance in front of me.

"Boys." I turned away from the gull. Ranger Johnson was on the beach. Immediately, my throat shrank. How long had he been around? What had he heard?

"What's going on here?" he asked. He looked terrible. The sweat rings and eye twitch were still there, but now he had bags under his eyes, like he hadn't slept in days. I could relate.

"Capture the flag, sir," I said, before Chris could launch into one of his verbal assaults. "I'm in jail," I added, without thinking about it. Maybe Chris's motormouth was contagious?

"Have you seen Grey?"

"No, sir," said Chris.

I shook my head. "Not since yesterday." The tide was coming in. Water lapped at my sneakers, forcing me to step closer to the ranger.

"Yesterday?" Ranger Johnson's head snapped in my direction. "Where? When? What did she say?"

His intensity caused me to step back—right into an incoming wave, soaking my shoe. Chris raised an eyebrow at me. He knew about our fight, and what she said about her dad.

"Um . . ." I thought about what I could say. "I was taking a nap near the battlements. She woke me up, gave me a Coke, we talked for a few minutes, then she left."

Ranger Johnson's eye stopped twitching. His stare bored into me like a hot drill.

"What did you talk about?"

I gulped. "Not much. She was annoyed," I said, hoping honesty would buy me reprieve from his stare. "Why?"

He ran his hands through his hair, raising it into spiky clumps.

"I need to take away her boat," he muttered. Before he could say more, screaming and cheers came from the path. We turned.

Derek burst onto the beach, holding my team's flag over his head like a Day-Glo victory banner. "Whoo! Winners!" he shouted—only it came out like "winnahz."

"Ollie-ollie yo go free," he jeered. "We kicked your team's butt.

"Sir," he said, noticing Ranger Johnson. "Um . . ."

Ranger Johnson waved him off and turned back to me.

"Next time you see Grey, tell her I need to speak with her. Immediately."

"Yes, sir," I responded. Chris had wandered over to celebrate with Derek and the rest of his team, which was streaming onto the beach.

Ranger Johnson stepped closer to me. "I'm going back to Gallops, Ollie. I haven't forgotten."

My stomach rolled in a tight ball, but I hoped he couldn't tell how nervous I was. I shrugged, not trusting myself to speak. He gave me one more hot-drill stare, and stalked off.

Crap.

27

I begged, pleaded, and even tried to bribe Chris into making another midnight cruise to Gallops while we cleaned up from dinner; he wasn't having it.

"No way!" he said through gritted teeth. "Dude, are you *insane?* Even I'm not that nuts. We got lucky. The sign is not that big a deal. The dia—err, rocks—are put away, and if we go back we'll get caught. Seriously. I'm willing to do that for something awesome, but not for a stupid *sign.* If he finds out, we tell the truth about finding the rocks."

I sighed. He was right—I knew it—but the not-going, not-fixing worried me. I had no idea what Ranger Johnson was up to, beyond wanting the diamonds, and as long as I hadn't covered my tracks, there was a possibility that I'd mess everything up.

I turned my back on Chris, scooped some sand into the frying pan, and rubbed it clean with a cloth. It was almost funny: A month ago, I couldn't leave my house without my parents' permission, and now I was trying to convince someone to sneak out in the middle of the night and *steal a boat. For a second time.* Who was this Ollie?!

I didn't know, but I kinda liked him. I grinned in spite of myself.

Chris finished packing the dinner supplies.

"I'm done," he said. I knew what he really meant.

"Guys, come to the fire pit," Mr. Fuentes called.

I stashed the frying pan and followed Chris to the group.

"I have several announcements: First, as you may have guessed, Dr. Gupta will not be returning to camp. The hospital needs him to stay for a major surgery tomorrow." Any hope I had of reaching the FBI before we hit land evaporated. Mr. F. went on, "Second, the Coast Guard notified me that we have a storm coming our way on Thursday night."

"What day is today?" Steve called. Everyone laughed. So did Mr. Fuentes.

"Tuesday," he responded. "We're taking this seriously. There will be a lot of heavy rain, and we're keeping an eye on the forecast in case packing up is a safer option. I want all of you to pack your belongings tomorrow, just in case we decide to leave early. Leave out only the essentials for the next couple of days."

There were some groans—packing up sucks, and no one wanted to do it before he had to—and then guys drifted away from the campfire.

Derek hung back, waiting for me. He fell into step beside me.

"Good takedown of Manuel," he said, poking me in the ribs. It hurt, but I didn't say anything, which annoyed him, I think, because he watched me like he was expecting something and scowled when it didn't happen. "Who's next on your list?"

"Not your business," I responded.

"No?" We were outside of my tent. "You're wrong there. See, someone still has you, because I don't. And if you have you, well, that doesn't work right, right?"

Was this kid for real? Did he have any idea of how lame he sounded? I was tired of his shenanigans.

"I don't have myself, DB. Beat it. Go tag someone so you can get my name and we can get this over with."

Derek scowled. "You are so dead."

"Whatever," I said, and pushed through the flap of my tent.

DAY 12

CHRIS'S GOTCHA! ALIVE/TAGGED LIST

STEVE

D-BAG DEREK

~~ME (CHRIS)~~

JACK

~~MANNY~~

~~DOUG~~ (left camp)

~~PETE~~

~~HORATIO~~

CAM

~~JORGE~~

RAVI

OLLIE

28

I slept like I was dead. Manny left for his swim and came back and I didn't hear a thing. They could've seen that he was missing, then sent out search helicopters and dogs and I wouldn't have moved.

When I woke up I realized that we had three days left in camp, then we'd get off this island and I could tell Agent Goh about the diamonds and—hopefully—get back to my normal life.

Or whatever normal was now.

Across the tent, Jack hurled Chris's Cape Cod T-shirt at him. He was stuffing his gear in his backpack, per Mr. Fuentes's orders the night before.

"What's this?" Chris peeled the T-shirt off his face. Manny and I were already hysterically laughing when Chris realized that it was the shirt Jack had worn after we found him on the beach, when Steve and Derek had stolen his clothes.

"Oh! Gross! You little—" Chris sputtered.

"Just returning your shirt, buddy." Jack cracked up. Manny high-fived me and Jack. Manny'd finally thawed. Chris raced out of the tent to wash his face. There could not be water hot enough for that.

Manny and I packed too. Grimy T-shirts, shorts, socks . . . my mom was going to hate my laundry bag when I got home. Manny held up a pair of filthy cargo shorts.

"These yours?" I nodded, and he balled them up. "Somethin' in the pocket, man." He turned the shorts over, about to open them, and then I remembered—the diamonds!

"Don't open it!" It came out sharper than I intended. Manny froze. "It's just my inhaler," I said, trying to cover up. I reached for them.

He tossed them, gently, and shrugged. "Doesn't feel like an inhaler," he said.

"Oh. It's just some . . . mints," I improvised. Lamely. I fished the tin out of the pocket and waved it in front of him, not opening it. "I wondered where it went."

Manny didn't believe me at all, I could tell. But he kept his mouth shut and finished packing. I stuffed the box in my shorts pocket. So much for the thaw.

On the way to breakfast, Steve, next to Ravi and me, staggered dramatically. I thought he was going to faint or something, and I reached out to catch him. He fell, heavy, into Ravi's arms.

"I. Can't. Go. On," Steve gasped. Pete and Horatio came to see what the commotion was about. I felt sick, but couldn't move or yell for help. Why wasn't anyone *doing* anything?

And then—the red sticker. Steve plunged it over his heart, letting out a death rattle that would make a casting director jealous. He closed his eyes.

"Jerk!" Ravi said. He opened his eyes and laughed hysterically. The other guys clapped, then wandered to breakfast.

"Can't tag a buddy," he said. He'd killed Jack last night, after dinner and gotten Ravi—Jack's target.

"So what now?" I asked. Would that affect the terms of my deal with Derek? I was supposed to tag Steve.

Steve stood and brushed himself off. "Now whoever had me gets Ravi."

During the morning meeting, Ravi signed up for storm preparedness. A group was going to look at the docks, seawalls, and structures on the island to make sure they weren't in danger from a strong storm. As much as I needed to get Ravi, storm readiness just wasn't my thing. I joined the orienteering group, hoping to spot my target while I was roaming around the island.

Instead of dismissing us, Mr. Fuentes kept looking at his watch.

"Okay, let's get started," he said. "Ollie has set up several caches around the fort." I directed the orienteering group to go to the first coordinate point. The scouts took off. I lingered, knowing there was more to this than he let on.

"You guys," he said to the storm preparedness group, "Ranger Johnson is supposed to take you to specific sites on the islands, but he's not here yet. I have a list, and I'll bring you to the first couple. He can catch up." He pursed his lips like my Bà does when she's upset.

The group shuffled off. Where was Ranger Johnson? And what kind of mood would he be in when he got back?

I glanced at the scouts' retreating backs. A split-second decision: Let Chris lead orienteering, head for the dock.

I'd tag Ravi, then find Ranger Johnson before he found me.

* * *

Steve, Derek, Pete, and Ravi were tightening the cleat screws on the boat dock. Mr. Fuentes stood on the beach, scowling, cell phone raised like a torch, trying to find a signal. Even from my spot in the shade at the edge of the path, I caught his frustration. Ranger Johnson's Park Service skiff was nowhere to be seen.

I stepped back into the woods to figure out my next move. I couldn't rush out there and tag Ravi—playing Gotcha! during sessions wasn't allowed, for one, and two, there was no good cover. He'd see me coming.

I'd have to catch him on his way to the next storm check site, and just hope that there'd be enough distance between him and Mr. Fuentes so I wouldn't get caught.

While I waited for them to finish, I sat on a patch of sea grass and took the diamonds from my pocket. They clicked against one another in the tin—a sound I could clearly hear over the waves, bird calls, and shouts of the guys on the beach.

Immediately, I thought of the old Jack and the Beanstalk fairy tale. My mom told it to me all the time when I was a kid. The story of Jack, the magic beans, and the plant that led him to the giant's lair fascinated and terrified me at the same time. The summer I was six my parents planted plain old green beans in our garden, and every morning I woke up anxious and excited to see if they'd sprouted to the sky.

Now I knew that magic beans didn't exist, but what I was holding was a pretty close second.

I opened the tin. Pouring the diamonds out would be a bad

idea—what if I lost one?—but holding one, or just feeling them, would be okay.

I reached in and used two fingers and a thumb to pull out one of the "rocks."

I closed my fist around it, then closed the tin. I set the secure package on the ground next to me.

I opened my palm.

The diamond glinted dully in the light, its milky surface doing its best to sparkle. This was real-life treasure. The best cache *ever*. It occurred to me to mark this moment—where I was when I held pirate treasure. I pulled my GPS from my pocket and jotted the coordinates down in my notebook.

". . . over to the fort?" Derek's voice was a lot closer than it had been when he was on the dock.

I scrambled to my feet, stuffing the diamond and GPS deep into my pocket. The guys were heading straight for the path—and me.

I stepped farther into the brush and crouched down. I'd forgotten to put on bug spray before I left the tent, and the little flies and mosquitoes were unbearable in here. One landed on my arm, but I didn't dare swat it in case the movement attracted attention. I breathed through my mouth, trying to be as quiet as possible.

"I gotta take a leak," Pete said. "I'll catch up."

"Watch what you water," Steve joked. Pete gave him the finger.

For a second, my heart was in my throat. I thought for sure that Poison Ivy Pete was going to cross off the path on my side of the woods. Instead, he went to the other side. When his back was to me and I was sure he was . . . occupied, I scooted onto the path behind Steve, Ravi, and Derek.

Gotcha! sticker in hand, I stayed back as far as I dared and hoped that Pete had had a lot of water this morning. The path split, and the guys went straight, toward the fort. I knew that the fork to the left skirted more of the island, but I could loop back and—if I was quick enough—get in front of them. Although sneaking up on Ravi would be the easiest way to get him out, I kind of wanted the challenge of coming head-on—and besides, there'd be less chance that Poison Ivy would come up behind me and ruin the whole thing. I went left.

I walked as fast as I dared, my aching muscles crying with every step. At least the breeze was back.

The path dipped down, away from the center of the island, back to the beach. If I was going to cut across, it would be here. I left the path and headed straight through the bramble-filled brush, mosquitoes and gnats dogging me like they had me in Gotcha!

After another minute, the gray granite wall of Fort Standish appeared through the trees. I slowed my pace, swatted a few more bugs, and came out of the woods on the far side of the fort from where Derek, Ravi, and Steve would approach. I stopped. Their voices were audible, but not clear enough to make out what they were saying. I'd beaten them to the fort.

Thrilled with the luck, I stayed close to the edge of the wall, edging my way around the fort's perimeter. The entrance gaped farther down, on the right.

Ravi's Red Sox shirt appeared through the trees at the head of path, just beyond it.

I ran for the darkened doorway, getting inside just before the guys stepped into the clearing around the fort. My chest tightened and I tried to control the wheezing.

They stood to my right, outside the door, waiting for Pete.

"What the hell?" Steve said. "Did he drink a gallon of water? Guy is *slow.*"

"No kidding—"

"Yeaaahhhh!" I yelled, jumping out from my hiding spot. The guys' faces wore matching expressions of shock. Before they could react, I dove at Ravi, sticking him right over the heart. "Gotcha!" My momentum carried me forward and he took a step back, right into the wall of the fort.

He stared down at his chest like he'd received an actual wound.

"You little—"

But I didn't hear him, because I was in my own state of shock. I'd never put the box of diamonds back in my pocket.

29

Before Ravi could hand over the slip for my next tag, I bolted for the trees. The only thing that mattered was that tin of diamonds. They were proof of what we found. Agent Goh would need them. Ranger Johnson couldn't have them.

My heart pounded, chest squeezed. I ignored the boa constrictor wrapping itself around my torso and just went down the path as fast as possible. Derek and Steve called out to me, but I just kept going. It didn't matter if they were behind me. Nothing did.

How could I have been so *stupid*?

The path thinned; I was nearing the beach. I slowed down, not wanting to miss the spot, and tried to breathe. The snake loosened its hold around my torso and air came a little easier.

I scanned the ground, and the edge of the path, trying to pinpoint where I sat. No mints box in sight. Then I remembered: My GPS! I'd marked the exact spot.

I pulled it out and retrieved the coordinates from my notebook. While I waited for it to do its satellite-thing, I cast my eyes around some more. Sea grass, leaves and beach sand, rocks, shells . . . no tin. I hoped I'd overshot it. And really, I hadn't been gone very long. Who could've come by?

I tried not to think of all the hikers and day visitors who came through this side of the island. Even though there was no one around right now, someone could have come through and picked it up. But I would've seen them on the path . . .

The GPS beeped. It pointed to my left. I was a few paces off. When I was in the right spot, the machine blinked at me. I crouched down, feeling the ground as well as looking at it. The container wasn't there.

Panic rose in my throat and I tried to control it. Maybe I'd kicked it when I stood? Maybe it was under a rock?

I was on my hands and knees, combing the ground like I was looking for, well, diamonds.

Nothing.

"Doc, what's the deal?" Derek came through the trees behind me. "What the heck are you doing?"

I sat back on my heels and wiped sweat from my brow. "Nothing. I'm looking for something. I dropped something." My words came out fast, blurred together.

"What?" he eyed me, suspicious.

"This?" Behind Derek was Ranger Johnson, hand raised, the small box nestled in his palm. "Is this what you boys are looking for?"

My heart thudded. That boa constrictor was back, and my airway clamped shut. It was all I could do to nod.

I forced myself to move. I pushed past Derek, and went straight up to Ranger Johnson.

"That's mine." I held my hand out, and he pulled the tin away.

"Littering on the islands is punishable by a fine, you know."

His voice sounded sharp and mean, but the eye twitch and sweat stains were still there. He was stressed out. Really stressed out.

"Sorry, sir," I said. "I wasn't littering. I was waiting for my friends"—I glanced at Derek, who to his credit, kept his mouth shut—"and I dropped that by accident. I came back here to pick it up."

Ranger Johnson's eyes flickered from me to Derek, who shrugged and nodded.

"Fine," he said. "But let's just make sure there's nothing against the rules in here, shall we?"

I gulped. "I'd rather you didn't," I said. "It's private."

Ranger Johnson raised an eyebrow at me and ignored my plea. He lifted the lid and I held my breath.

He tilted it.

We heard the clicking before we saw the diamonds. There were enough still in the box to fill his palm. If I was going to tell him the truth, that Grey, Chris, and I found them, now would be the time. But I just couldn't. I didn't trust him.

"What the—?" Derek said.

"See? Just some beach quartz," I said, using the most fake cheerful tone I could possibly muster. My voice sounded high and thin and unbelievable to my own ears. "I'll take that back now."

Ranger Johnson stared at the diamonds like they were magic beans that he'd just traded his last cow for.

"These are yours?" he asked, not taking his eyes off them.

"I found them," I said, thinking as fast as I could, "on the day that we were doing the wildlife census. They're just sea glass or quartz or something. I thought they'd look cool in my room back home."

Derek had been silent the whole time, also staring at the rocks in Ranger Johnson's hand. You *could* believe they were sea glass—some were milky and none of them sparkled like what you'd find in an engagement ring—but you'd have to work really hard to believe they were worthless.

"If those are beach glass, then my left leg is a candy cane," Derek finally said.

"Exactly," said Ranger Johnson. He seemed to have recovered from the shock. "Ollie, this is serious. Federal Regulation number 311B says you can't remove anything from the parks. And we both know you didn't find them on this island. And we *all* know what these are—some of Long Ben Avery's diamonds, which belong in a museum, *not* in a box that held breath mints. So tell me, where *did* you find them?" His voice was deadly even.

I am no idiot. There was no such thing as Federal Regulation number 311B. I had to learn all kinds of random rules when I first started caching, so I knew what was okay and what to avoid.

But I am no idiot.

"On Gallops." I pointed to the far side of the island, away from the retaining wall. "I found them in a cave [true] in a rotted bag on the floor [lie]. I assumed they were sea glass [also a lie]."

"You need to tell me *exactly* where you found them. There may be more." Ranger Johnson's eyes had a funny, excited glow. Even the twitch had stopped. "Where were you?" He directed that part to Derek.

"I had no part in this," he said. "I'm not going to get in trouble

213

for something this little weasel did." Ranger Johnson gave him a skeptical look, but turned back to me.

"Where?" his voice was edgy.

"Past the beach," I said. "Closest to the salt marsh." That would give him something to do. That stretch of beach was really rocky and it would be difficult to search.

He gave a curt nod, then poured the diamonds back in the box, clicked the lid closed, and put it in a pocket of his shorts. "I'll take care of these, thank you."

My stomach rolled. I couldn't believe how stupid I'd been. Having one diamond in my pocket probably wasn't proof enough for Agent Goh.

"Get back to camp. Both of you. You're lucky I'm not saying anything to Mr. Fuentes about this." He spun on his heel and left us staring after him.

"Way to go, Doc Watson," sneered Derek. "You just lost yourself a fortune."

Derek dogged me all the way back to the campsite, trying to get me to tell him more about the diamonds and where I found them.

I ignored him, instead focusing on not throwing up and on how I was going to break the news to Chris. *How could I have been so stupid?*

The site was empty. I went into our tent, Derek on my heels.

"Back off," I said.

"I'm just trying to help."

"Yeah, right." I glared at him until he left.

I tried to lie on my sleeping bag, but I was too fidgety and my brain wouldn't stop. I rehashed every step of the morning: packing with Manny, getting the diamonds from the old pair of shorts . . . and each time I got to the part where I left the diamonds behind, I started over, hoping that magically I could change the past. Didn't happen.

I stood, but didn't have anywhere to go. Pacing didn't work—there was no room in the tent. Instead, I settled for standing next to my sleeping bag, fiddling with the buttons on my GPS. I erased all the data, then reentered some coordinates I knew from memory: my house in Jamaica Plain, Moxie's house, our junior high . . . the rhythmic pressing of the buttons helped straighten my head out. And would prevent anyone from finding the location of the remaining diamonds.

Was what had happened really so terrible? Yes, I'd let Ranger Johnson have the tin of diamonds, but I still had one in my pocket—and I knew where the rest were. I hadn't told him anything about the others, so those were still safe. As a matter of fact, having the diamonds might make him chill out a little. Grey said he kept asking about them; maybe he'd think that was all of them. There was no way he knew how many were actually part of Long Ben Avery's treasure, so he could search more or sell or give them to the person on the phone, whatever. And besides, we were still going to tell the authorities about the rest. The ranger even said he wasn't going to tell Mr. Fuentes—basically, I wouldn't get in trouble at all. So there was nothing to worry about, right?

I had to believe that.

* * *

Right before lunch, Chris, who'd led the orienteering group, came into the tent and fished around his backpack for another layer, talking all the while.

"You're not gonna believe how long it took the guys to find the caches you hid, Ols. I mean, seriously, they were so lame. It's like they'd never used a compass, ya know? So pathetic . . ."

I raised my hand.

"I screwed up," I told him. "Royally."

He paused, one hand hanging on to a sleeve that stuck out from the bag, like he was holding hands with someone inside his backpack.

I told him what happened with Ranger Johnson, the diamonds, and Derek.

"And so he has them, and Derek knows we found them, and now he's not going to leave me alone," I finished.

"Awesome," groaned Chris. "Just what we need." He pulled the long-sleeved T-shirt over his head and his existing shirt.

"But," I added, realizing something only after hearing myself tell the story, "it proves that Ranger Johnson is totally up to something sketchy, because he is keeping it from Mr. Fuentes. And we hid the rest, remember? He won't be able to find them."

"Maybe because it doesn't matter what Mr. Fuentes does or if the ranger finds them," Chris threw in. "If it's really a federal situation."

"I doubt it," I responded. I had a tiny bit of experience with finding things that didn't belong to me, and *everyone* has an interest in them.

"Are you sure we shouldn't just tell Mr. F.? He could help us, I know it."

I rubbed my head. "Chris, what could we *actually* tell him? That the ranger asked us to search for treasure, but we went to Gallops alone, at night, and found it?"

"No!" he protested. "We leave out that part, and just tell him that we found the diamonds when you hurt your arm. Let him figure out what to do with the ranger. I mean, I'm sure Mr. F. would let you call the FBI . . ."

Chris had a point. Agent Goh had warned me to stay out of trouble, and this did not qualify as trouble-free.

"Fine. You win. We tell him. Together. When it's quiet." Chris grinned and visibly relaxed. I hadn't realized how much strain this had put on him too.

"What about Grey?" he asked.

"Grey is going to explode when she finds out." While we were talking, I found a Death-Star-shaped pencil sharpener in the bottom of my backpack. I dumped the shavings in a corner of the tent.

The whistle sounded from the fire pit. "Scouts!" called Mr. Fuentes. "Meeting!"

I popped the diamond in the empty pencil sharpener and clicked it closed. I'd guard this one with my life.

30

"I have some disappointing news," Mr. Fuentes began, before lunch. "Ranger Johnson is ill and won't be able to lead this afternoon's fishing expedition. Instead, we're going to stay here and work on a variety of badge skills. Older scouts will set up stations and the younger ones will rotate through."

Everyone groaned because we'd be stuck in the campsite for the rest of the day.

My groan was because I knew that the only thing wrong with Ranger Johnson was a fistful of diamonds.

"Ollie! You need to work on your wood-carving badge," Mr. Fuentes read off a sheet. "You're at Horatio's station."

I'd avoided this badge forever because I was afraid I'd cut my hand open, á la Doug with the hatchet, plus, I was pretty sure that with everything that was on my mind, I'd lose all five fingers in less than five minutes.

Jack joined us, and Horatio handed us knives and told us to find a branch to carve.

Surprisingly, once he showed me the way to hold the knife and the wood so as *not* to cut off all my fingers, I kind of liked it. My carving looked more like a cow than a dog, but whatever. It was good to focus on something else for a while, even though I was still working out when Chris and I would tell Mr. F. about everything that had been going on.

Jack, who made a whistle, was amazingly good at carving. He went to find another branch.

"I'm supposed to give you this." Horatio slid a slip of paper to me across the log we were sitting on.

I recognized it immediately: my next kill. From Ravi.

I sighed and turned it over:

Derek.

In spite of everything that had happened that day, seeing his name on the sheet brought a smile to my face.

I was supposed to go down. I was supposed to let Derek win.

I didn't care about his rules anymore.

DAY 13

CHRIS'S GOTCHA! ALIVE/TAGGED LIST

~~STEVE~~

D-BAG DEREK

~~ME (CHRIS)~~

~~JACK~~

~~MANNY~~

~~DOUG~~ (left camp)

~~PETE~~

~~HORATIO~~

CAM

~~JORGE~~

~~RAVI~~

OLLIE

31

After a morning spent doing more badge classes and swimming the beach, everyone was bored. Mr. Fuentes hadn't heard from Ranger Johnson again, and he'd been so busy running the camp himself that Chris and I hadn't had a chance to get him alone. Had the ranger skipped town with Grey and the diamonds? Or had she taken him to Gallops to show him the cave?

We finished lunch, and Mr. Fuentes looked at us. He rubbed his head with his hands.

"I don't know what's up with Ranger Johnson," he began, "but we have a few things left that we need to do before we leave."

He explained that the troop always did a cleanup of Fort Standish, raking out leaves and clearing debris as a thank-you to the Parks Service for letting us camp for a reduced fee.

"Since there's a storm coming tonight, we'll go ahead and do that today," he finished.

Derek cleared his throat.

"Mr. F.? Um, aren't you forgetting something?"

Mr. Fuentes sighed. "Really, Derek? I think we've had enough to deal with these past two weeks. Do we really need to do this?"

"But it's tradition!" Derek exclaimed. "You can't mess with troop tradition!"

I had no idea what he was talking about. Chris must've been able to tell that from my expression, because he leaned over and said, low, "Derek's talking about our annual game of flashlight tag. We play it on the last night of camp."

More games? At first, I was annoyed, and then I realized that it was also a perfect opportunity for me to tag Derek in Gotcha! Cam was still in play too, which meant Derek had him.

I just had to get to Derek before Cam got me.

We broke down lunch and traipsed to the fort for our service project. I worked with Chris and Manny on clearing leaves from the south side. Jack was inside—he wanted to be in the shade.

Every few minutes, I stuck my hand in my pocket, checking for the diamond in the Death Star. After yesterday's colossal mess-up, I had to protect what we had left. It had added another layer to my paranoia.

"What is going on in your pants?" Manny asked. He leaned on his rake, letting Chris and me go on without him. I stopped too, and wiped my forehead.

"What're you lookin' at my pants for?"

He shrugged. "You've got your hand in your pocket like there's treasure in there or somethin'."

Chris stopped. We exchanged a quick glance.

"You're lookin' at his pants, he's not raking, I'm doing all the work over here," Chris said. "Seems like I'm getting the bad end of the deal. Maybe I'll just take a nap until you're done discussing what's in Ollie's pants."

Manny made a rude gesture at Chris, who threw a rock at his

feet, and they started horsing around. Chris's talent for distraction was amazing.

We were almost done with our section of the fort when Ranger Johnson came out of the woods. When my dad is shocked he says he couldn't be more surprised if he woke up with his head sewn to the carpet.

I was that surprised.

But at first it was like the ranger didn't see us. As he got closer, I was amazed at how terrible he looked: His eyes were all sunken, with dark purple smudges underneath them. He hadn't shaved, and his face seemed raw and irritated. Those sweat stains were back under his armpits, and his whole uniform was wrinkled like he'd slept in it—or hadn't slept at all, but left it on.

The guy had a box of diamonds and he *still* couldn't get it together? This was way worse than I thought.

"You lied to me. I've been on south beach, and I can't find the cave," he directed at me. "Are you sure that's where you found them?"

"Yes, sir," I said. Had he been on the beach all night? Looking for more diamonds? The thought, combined with Ranger Johnson's appearance, made me uncomfortable—like I was to blame for whatever was going on with him. And where was Grey, if he'd been out all night? Was her mom home?

"Where's Grey?" I asked, feeling bold.

"Grey?" He waved a hand dismissively. "She's home."

"Is she okay?" I tried.

"She's all right," he muttered. He turned away from us and followed the wall of the fort toward the back of the island.

"Weird," I said.

"Really weird," Chris echoed.

"What was he looking for?" Manny asked. "He acted like you knew."

"He acted like a lot of things, Manny. None of which made sense. C'mon, let's get this finished up. I'm done with this place."

We cleared the rest of the leaves in silence. And all I could think about was the ranger. And Grey. Was he telling the truth?

Manny told Mr. Fuentes that we'd seen Ranger Johnson, but when Mr. Fuentes got a good signal and called him, he still didn't answer his phone.

But it didn't seem to matter to Mr. Fuentes anymore. The boat to take us home would be coming the next afternoon, and most of the morning would be spent breaking down camp. He gave us instructions about breakdown over dinner, then added casually, like he wasn't thinking about it all afternoon, "Since you guys did such a great job around Fort Standish, you can play flashlight tag tonight."

Everyone cheered.

"Wait!" He raised his hand for silence. "We *are* expected to get a big storm, so as soon as the first indicator of bad weather hits—a raindrop, a roll of thunder, whatever—you are all required to bunk down. Got me?"

"Gotcha!" Chris answered for all of us, and we cracked up.

I looked around at the guys I'd spent the past two weeks with. Although I'd come here under not-great circumstances, and run into another weird situation, I was glad that I'd gone provo. These were good guys. Not Derek—he was a jerk—but Chris and Manny and Jack were cool. Since Chris and Manny would also be going to Chestnut Prep in September, I'd get to hang out with them after this was all over.

After I told the FBI about the diamonds we'd found.

We broke down dinner and I was back on pot-scrubbing duty. I couldn't stop thinking about how weird Ranger Johnson had been acting, and how bad he looked. And on the heels of that were thoughts about Grey. I hadn't seen her since our fight, and that had been a couple of days ago. I'd figured that she was so ticked off at me that she'd been avoiding me, but what if there was something else going on? Did the ranger tell her that he had the diamonds?

Manny nudged me. "Dude, you've been scrubbing the same pan for the past five minutes. These are cheap, yo—you'll wear a hole in it."

"Sorry." I put the pan in the plastic bin where we kept the supplies, my mind still on Grey. Something wasn't right, and I couldn't figure out what I was missing.

"Earth to Ollie," Manny continued. "You are such a space shot. Derek'll get you out in no time tonight if you don't get it together. So get it together."

It was the warmest Manny had been to me since I'd snapped at him over the mints tin.

"We cool?" I tried.

He grinned. "We're cool."

Feeling better, I pushed thoughts of Grey to the back of my

mind. Her dad had said she was fine after all. The next step: Finishing Gotcha! and getting Derek back. And after flashlight tag? Well, maybe Chris and I could finally spill this whole mess to Mr. F.

It was good to have a plan.

After cleanup, around sunset, we did a flashlight check. Dark clouds clumped together on the far side of the harbor, conspiring to eat up the clear sky that had hung over Lovells for the past two weeks.

"Be mindful," Mr. Fuentes said, pointing up. "You guys aren't going to have a ton of time out there. I'm going to restrict you to this side of the island. Fort Standish is your northern border, the edge of the marsh is the western, and the last set of gun batteries is the eastern. Pier, north beach—off limits. Got it?"

We nodded.

"Camp is base. You get tagged, you come back here. You go with a partner. One of you gets out, you're both back here."

"C'mon, Mr. F.!" Derek complained, "We always play every man for himself. Partners is lame."

Mr. Fuentes shook his head and pointed to the sky again. "You're lucky you're playing at all. I'm here by myself, remember? Partners," he said firmly. "I'll give you ten minutes to hide. Whistle means game on." He blasted a tweet on the police whistle. Yup, we'd be able to hear that all the way at the batteries. "Whistle also means game off. Two blasts: Come in immediately. Got it?"

"Got it," we responded.

"Get your partner and—go!"

Chris and I took off toward Fort Standish and the gun batteries. Manny and Jack headed toward the beach, and Derek and Steve went east, toward the far side of the island. There were only woods in that direction, so I wasn't sure what their plan was.

Chris and I were going to use the fort to protect our back, and range out from there, searching for scouts. The sun was going down, and long shadows reached toward us, making the edge of the path hard to see.

"So I heard Horatio and Cam talking about Gotcha! and that Derek tagged Cam, but bribed him to keep it on the down low so you'd think he was still in play. So you've gotta watch out."

I wasn't surprised at what Derek pulled. But I was going to try my hardest to get him out. He couldn't prove we'd stolen the boats, and we were leaving tomorrow. Game over.

"Can you believe we'll be able to make that call tomorrow?" Chris said. "I mean, it's felt like forever, but tomorrow we'll be *done*. Do you think Mr. F. will flip out when we tell him? How do you want to start?"

"You start," I said absently. Something was still bothering me, but we'd found an alcove where we could see anyone coming, and waited for the whistle to signal the beginning of the game.

Off to our left there were footsteps and low voices. Another team had the same idea. Chris and I pressed into the wall and waited, silent.

The team decided that they were safe too, and waited out the whistle.

It was nearly full dark, and my eyes strained to make Chris

out, even in the small space. Dusk is the worst time of day for me—even with my glasses, the world looks flat and two dimensional—so I looked forward to full dark, when my eyes would adjust better.

Twweeeeeeeeeeet!

Chris leaned over, his breath smelling like hot dogs. "Let's get those guys before they know what hit 'em."

Game on.

I patted my pocket: inhaler. Cool.

I nodded at Chris, but he probably couldn't see me.

"Let's go."

The other team was to our left. We'd need to come out of our alcove quietly and quickly, so we could tag them before they got us.

"Get low," Chris said. I crouched, and we half ran, half waddled out from our spot. The trees created deep black pools of shadow against the navy dusk. The sky was lighter, but not by much—and the clouds would eat that up soon.

We stayed under the trees, away from the side of the fort, and kept our footsteps muffled. My heart pounded, and a tingle of excitement skittered through my body. Was I becoming an adrenaline junkie?

Even my weak eyes spotted the other team. Their silhouettes were darker against the gray of the fort. Not a good tactic.

I readied my flashlight and squeezed Chris's arm: *One. Two. Three!*

We clicked our lights on right at the other guys. The beams

stabbed them in the face and chest, cutting a yellow-white streak through the night.

Horatio and his partner Jorge. These were older scouts, who should've known better than to . . .

"It's a trap!" I said to Chris. As soon as the words were out of my mouth, I heard the crashing in the brush. Derek and Steve had looped back to the fort, the same way that I had when I'd tagged Steve.

"Run!" Chris yelled.

We veered deeper into the woods, where, although we could be heard for miles, the shadows were darker and it'd be harder for them to get a tag. The guys crashed through the brush behind us, and the more I ran, the more my chest started to tighten. There was no way I was going to be able to outrun these guys.

We were coming up on a big tree that had tipped over at the root, creating a deep pit. I grabbed Chris and pointed to it. When we got close, I jumped in, hoping that there was nothing alive or possibly impaling in there.

I slid down the side and hit bottom. It was shallower than I thought. I scrambled toward the roots, trying to ignore the tickle of what I hoped were dead tree parts and not crawly residents in my hair.

Chris flattened out across the bottom. We were pinned down. All Derek and Steve had to do was shine their lights in there, and we'd be out of the game.

Thunder rumbled. The ground under me vibrated with the noise.

Two tweets from Mr. Fuentes's police whistle followed. Game over.

Derek and Steve stopped running not far from where we were hiding. We stayed still.

"Crap," Derek said. "I wanted to get those little wanks."

"Sucks," Steve agreed. "Wanna split up on the way back? We can corner them and you can get your Gotcha! victory."

Derek was silent for a second. "Yeah," he said finally. "Let's get this over with. I'm sick of chasing the tiny turds."

They moved off. Chris and I waited for what felt like minutes, but was probably only thirty seconds, then we crawled out. We had to be on guard on the walk back to the campsite, but get there quickly so Mr. Fuentes wouldn't be mad.

Thunder rumbled again, and lightning streaked across the sky. A big, warm drop of rain splashed on my head. Then another. Three steps later and the skies opened up. Chris and I were drenched in seconds.

"Let's go!" Chris called over the gush of rain. It pounded on the leaves, created puddles at our feet, and changed from warm to freezing.

I didn't care about Derek finding me, and I was sure he didn't care about anything other than getting back either.

Which is why I was shocked when found myself flying through the rain and landing face-first in the mud. Derek had tripped me.

I scrambled for my glasses; he clicked his flashlight on. The Gotcha! sticker was in his hand. I cleaned my glasses as best I could on my soaked and muddy T-shirt and put them on.

"I was hoping to get you in front of everyone," he said, "but now I just want to get this over with."

He stepped toward me and I pushed back along the ground. Cold mud oozed into the top of my shorts.

"Hey, DB!" Chris flicked his flashlight on, and when Derek turned to him, Chris pitched a mud-ball right at Derek's head. I climbed to my feet.

A spotlight hit all three of us.

"You three are coming with me."

It was Ranger Johnson. And he was holding a flare gun, pointed right at us.

32

"Let's go!" He gestured with the gun, sending us toward the beach path. "I can't figure it out, Ollie. I've been looking all over that beach where you found the diamonds, and I haven't seen that cave. Did you give me the right information? I doubt it," he answered, without waiting for me to go on.

"Sir, there must be some kind of mistake," Derek said. Did I look as miserable as he did: Sopping wet, muddy, and face as white as Jack's butt. "I'm not sure what you want with these guys, but I don't have any part in it. I was just—"

"Knock it off!" Ranger Johnson said. "Walk."

This was a completely different crazy than we'd seen earlier. Did he have some kind of multiple personality disorder? Maybe he didn't know what he was doing.

"You're going to show me where you found the diamonds," he said. "Grey told me."

"Grey *told?*" squeaked Chris, like he knew he should be quiet but he just couldn't.

With the sheeting rain and the rising winds, it was hard to see beyond the beam of Ranger Johnson's flashlight. Or should he be ex-Ranger Johnson? 'Cause I didn't think the Parks Service would let him keep his job after this.

If there was an "after this."

"Of course she told," he said.

"Where's Grey?" I said.

We'd come out onto the beach near the pier. Thunder slammed across the island, and lightning followed. It was so close, and the atmosphere was so charged, the hair on my arms and the back of my neck stood up.

"Never mind where she is," shouted Ranger Johnson. On the beach, the wind howled and the surf crashed. "I need the rest of those diamonds. And you're going to take me to them."

More thunder.

"What the heck diamonds are you talking about? The ones in that box?" asked Derek. "I'm not part of this. Let me go," he directed to Ranger Johnson.

"Shut up!" Johnson yelled. He swung his flare gun toward Derek. "You are *too* part of this. You know about the treasure. You looked for it. You wanted to find it."

"Everyone knows that story," Derek yelled. "Especially if you've gone to scout camp on the islands for almost ten years! And you made me look. I thought it was a joke!"

We were across the beach, and although I was fighting the whipping wind and driving rain, I could see where Ranger Johnson was taking us: a boat, tied to the pier. The waves slamming on shore roared, and the boat rocked like the Shake 'n' Barf ride at the carnival. My stomach heaved just looking at it.

"I know you lied," Ranger Johnson shouted. "I spent a whole day checking that stupid beach, and I remembered what you said about the No Trespassing sign. I went back there today. All the

No Trespassing signs are still up. So I asked Grey, and she told me about the *real* cave, and that you moved them. You're not going to tell me where those diamonds are, you're going to take me to them."

"No one needs to get hurt," I said, fishing through lines I'd heard in movies or on TV shows. "I can just tell you where they are and you can let us go. You don't want to take us with you. You don't want to even go over tonight. It's too dangerous."

"Danger? What do you know about *danger?*" he roared. "Those goons threatened my *daughter.*" His voice cracked. He turned his face to the sky, rain pelting down on it, and in the glow of his flashlight I could see how pasty and sick he looked. *What?* Who was he talking about? This must have been what was eating at him these past couple of days. Grey was in trouble. Or would be. Even though I didn't trust—or really *like*—Grey, I didn't want her to get hurt. I shivered, from the cold rain or the realization, I wasn't sure which.

"Go!" We were at the foot of the dock. Obediently, we stepped from the beach onto the wood, slippery from the rain.

"Mr. Fuentes will miss us," Derek said. "He'll come looking!"

"I don't care," said Ranger Johnson. Those words were the scariest yet. Scarier than the flare gun, even—well, flare guns aren't that scary. He could've said that Mr. F. would never find us, or that Mr. Fuentes thought he was home sick, or that everyone would assume we'd taken shelter from the storm in the fort—all things that were plausible. But he said he didn't care. Not good. Not good at all.

Chris caught my eye, and from his worried expression I could tell we were on the same page.

"Get in," Ranger Johnson said, stabbing his light at the wildly bobbing boat.

Derek, shivering and still an idiot, balked. "No way, dude."

"Get *in*!"

"The man has a gun, D," Chris pointed out.

"It's a *flare* gun," Derek said. His feet were planted.

Were, until Ranger Johnson gave him a shove.

Derek pinwheeled his arms, searching for balance in the air and rain, and staggered a step forward—and his foot skidded right off the edge of the dock.

I felt, more than heard, the *thwack* his head made when it slammed into the edge of the boat on the way down. Even Ranger Johnson winced.

Then came the splash.

"You killed him!" Chris screamed.

Ranger Johnson's white face turned green and slack, but he regained his composure. "You." He stabbed his light at Chris. "Get in there and get him. I saw your lifesaving scores. You." He stabbed me with the light. "Don't move."

This guy was seriously unstable. I nodded.

Chris peeled off a couple of his sodden layers, kicked off his shoes, moved out of the way of the bobbing boat, and did what he was told—he dove in after Derek. Ranger Johnson went to the edge of the pier to follow the action. I tried to look, but he demanded that I stay in the middle of the pier. Worried that the last person who knew where the diamonds were would get loose, I guess. I stayed where I was, surprisingly asthma-attack free. Guess I was getting used to people pointing guns at me this summer. Even flare guns.

"Bring him onshore!" Ranger Johnson called.

Well, at least Chris had found Derek. But I didn't see how he could get him through the smashing waves without help.

I was able to watch Chris when he moved farther away from the pier and turned toward shore. Chris must be a really strong swimmer, because he towed Derek's body through the surf like it was nothin'. Waves were breaking over his face at times, though, that's how high the whitecaps were.

Getting Derek out of the surf was tricky. Ranger Johnson moved to the edge of the water and told me to stay on the pier. Derek's head lolled, but his arm moved as Chris and Ranger Johnson dragged him onto the beach.

I let out a breath that I didn't even know I was holding.

Thunder rolled again. The next lightning flash illuminated Chris and Ranger Johnson dragging Derek back onto the pier.

Back onto the pier?!

They thumped him down a few yards away from me, and I raced over—taking care on the slick boards—to help.

Derek was unconscious, a big gash in his forehead from where he hit the boat on the way down. He was definitely breathing, but the cut was ugly. Chris was performing all the first aid that he'd ever learned—checking his airway, straightening his neck—and then he went for the pile of his discarded clothes. He pulled a T-shirt out, cursed that it wasn't dry, and asked me to help him tear it. At first, I didn't know what he was doing, then I realized he was making a bandage.

"Hold his head a little," he directed to me. And once again, I saw how good Chris was in certain situations—especially situations that forced him to concentrate on one task at a time.

Sopping and shivering, he tied the makeshift bandage tight. Thunder exploded overhead, and the wind whipped off the water.

"Ranger, sir, he's hurt bad. We gotta get him to a hospital," said Chris. He wiped rain, and probably tears, out of his eyes. He trembled. "C'mon. Look at him."

Ranger Johnson had been standing over us the whole time, not lifting a finger since they'd brought Derek onto the pier. Now he was biting his nails.

"Not until I get the diamonds," he said, staring straight at me.

"I'll tell you where they are. Exactly where they are," I added. Forget Agent Goh, forget whatever this guy wanted to do with them, no centuries-old pirate treasure was worth some kid bleeding to death on a dock—even if it was Derek.

"Not good enough," the ranger said. "You lied before. My little girl needs to stay safe. You're going to take me to them yourself." As he spoke, he knelt down and fished a black bag out of the bobbing boat. I'd missed the perfect opportunity to send him overboard. I wouldn't make that mistake twice.

He stood, two items in his hands. Lightning split the sky.

Duct tape and rope.

33

Ranger Johnson duct taped Chris's hands and feet together, then did the same to the unconscious Derek. To make sure they weren't going anywhere, he tied them together and then lashed them to a boat cleat on the pier. There was no way they could escape. And when—or if—they did, he and I would be at sea.

"Get in the boat," he told me. He slapped a piece of duct tape over Chris's mouth. "I've been wanting to do *that* since I met you, kid."

Above the tape, Chris's eyes were fearful. I didn't know what to do, so I just kind of nodded at him. He'd be okay.

I peered over the edge of the dock. This boat was a small motorboat, with one of those outboard motors that you tilt up in the back so you can run the boat up onto dry land.

Thunder rolled again, and the rain kept sheeting. I doubted I'd see dry land ever again.

I didn't know how to climb in. The boat pitched and rocked with the waves. There was no way I could get in there without killing myself.

And then Ranger Johnson nudged me with the flare gun.

I dropped my wet butt onto the soaking dock, dangled my feet over the edge, and dropped into the boat on the next big swell. For a nauseating second I was sure it was going to roll, but I slid to the middle of a bench seat and it steadied . . . then lurched at the next big wave. Had I been a better swimmer, I would've jumped. But my fear of what would happen to me in the water was greater than my fear of what would happen if I stayed in the boat.

Ranger Johnson hopped in doing pretty much the same thing. He tucked the gun in the waistband of his shorts while he got the motor in the water and tried to get it started.

"Untie us," he directed. I nodded, and unwrapped the line at the front cleat.

The engine coughed and caught, and he took off before I sat down. I stumbled backward, my back slamming the edge of the seat in a hot burst of pain and my butt landing in the pooled water in the bottom of the boat. I didn't think it was possible to get wetter, but I did.

The rain was pouring down from above, the ocean spraying salt water from the sides as the boat heaved over the waves. It was like being on one of those river raft rides—only in the ice cold, pitch-black, with a flare gun at your back.

Exactly like that.

I couldn't help it: I leaned over the side and puked.

It didn't make me feel any better. I wiped my mouth with the back of my hand.

"The diamonds are in one of the ruined buildings," I shouted. "In a blue-and-white-striped pillowcase."

"You'll show me where," Ranger Johnson yelled back. The boat jounced over a wave and my teeth clicked together, hard.

Spray mixed with the rain and splashed me in the face. Cold, miserable, and wet, I let tears join the rest of the water in the boat. How had I gotten here?

More importantly, how would I ever get out of this?

The lightning guided our way across the harbor. I kept reminding myself that Ranger Johnson had navigated these waters for a long time, and he wouldn't run us into a rock or buoy. But a glance back at him, sopping wet, staring into the distance like he didn't see me, or the island, or anything, wasn't reassuring.

Shivers wracked my body, making my back hurt even more.

"Hold on!" Ranger Johnson yelled all of a sudden.

Hold on to what? I grabbed the edge of the seat as the little boat was violently thrown forward once . . . twice . . . again. We were riding the surf in.

I'm no boating expert by any means, but I am pretty sure you're not ever-ever-ever-ever supposed to do that, because it can wreck the boat.

The ground scraped the bottom and the abrupt stop threw me forward. I caught the sides, hands slipping along the fiberglass, but stopped myself from falling face-first into the bench in front of me.

"Get out." Another nudge with the gun. I flopped over the side, landing up to my ankles in cold water. A wave pushed in, knocking me off balance. I scrabbled at the side of the boat as the strength of the water hit me like a Mini Cooper.

"Walk," he ordered. I slogged to the shore, the current sucking at my legs and every incoming wave threatening to take me out. Ranger Johnson's flashlight gave off a watery glow. I wasn't ready for him to know that I had one too. I hoped mine still worked.

We reached the beach, rain pelting us, and I stopped and crossed my arms in an effort to stay warm. I sneezed, never so happy to be on land.

"Let's go," he said. "Take me there."

"Where are the buildings?" I said. We were talking loudly. The crashing surf and wind hadn't let up at all. "I've only been here a couple of times."

"Which building?"

I looked at him blankly. "How should I know? It was just a foundation. A big one."

He swore. "Let's go to the hospital first. You tell me as soon as you know if it's the right one."

He walked in front of me, using his flashlight to lead the way. I followed him across the beach, my mind racing, trying to recall the topography of Gallops. Of course I knew exactly where the pillowcase was; I had to stall. Maybe Chris would be able to get out of that duct tape, or Mr. Fuentes had sent out a search party that'd find him and Derek.

And then what, Ollie? I asked myself. *How do you think a cavalry is going to get here, in this weather?*

I couldn't worry about that stuff.

We walked into the mown lawn area across from the beach. Ranger Johnson kept turning around to check on me, but I stayed really close to him. There was nowhere for me to go—yet.

His flashlight picked up the gray stone of a foundation in front of us. I pretended that I wasn't sure if it was the place, peering over the wall in a couple of different points, asking him to shine his flashlight into corners and down the stairs.

"This isn't it," I said finally.

He came over to me in three big steps and grabbed my sodden T-shirt. His fist on it was like squeezing out a washcloth. Water poured onto my sneakers.

"You better not be dinking around with me," he snarled. Water ran down his face in rivulets and his eyes were wild. "These people are not to be messed with. And neither am I."

"I'm not!" Terror hit my throat. My chest locked up. "Lemme go." He released my T-shirt and watched as I took a hit from my inhaler. Then he turned his back to me and ran his hands through his hair.

"I have to keep her safe," he said. His voice was hoarse. "You have no idea who these people *are*."

For a split second, I felt bad for the guy. I mean, someone was threatening Grey. He clearly had some issues going on at home. But he'd also kidnapped me—at flare-gunpoint—gotten Derek knocked out (maybe not so bad, but I'd feel terrible if anything *really* awful happened to him), and duct taped and tied one of my best friends to a pier.

Not an okay guy.

I looked up at him. "Let's go to the next building."

He nodded. We turned in the direction where his light pointed, and that's when I spotted it: a small white boat, off shore. It was behind one of the turns in the island. I hoped it was the Coast Guard, but I knew—*knew*—that it wasn't.

It was Grey's.

"Is that Grey's boat?" I yelled over the rain. Even he would think she was crazy for sailing—alone—in this weather.

He swore again. "I *told* her to stay home. Let's go. Hustle! Hustle!" We headed toward the beach, where the white boat was getting closer to shore. As we crossed the meadow, I stepped into a rabbit hole and my ankle turned. Something *snapped*, then let go. Pain shot across the outside of my foot.

"Come on, kid. Move," Ranger Johnson said. I'd paused to rub it and was waiting for the searing pain to go away. My eyes flooded with tears. Saying anything wouldn't help.

We kept going. Me, feeling like I'd stomped on a knife point with every step and trying to keep up; him, striding toward the beach like it was a lifeline.

Which, I suppose, it was.

Ranger Johnson seemed to forget about me as we approached the last bluff before the beach. He got a little ways in front of me. To my left was a thick stand of trees. There were buildings in there, and the little boat we'd come out in. Did I dare . . . ?

I waited for a few more seconds, when I was sure he was focused on his footing and not on me. And then I simply . . . turned and limped into the trees.

I went as fast as I could; heart pounding, pain wrapping itself around my foot like a boot. I hoped that he'd be so busy trying to get to Grey that he wouldn't notice my absence.

Finding a place to hide—a good place—was my only plan. If I found a good enough place, and the rain held up, I could maybe—maybe—last until help came.

What the heck was Grey doing here? Was she trying to find the diamonds? Did she know what her dad had planned for Chris, Derek, and me?

I slogged through the woods, listening for shouts or yells and expecting lights to shine on me at any second. But the rain was too loud for me to hear anything, which made me jittery. I just hoped that was working in my favor too.

Lightning streaked across the sky, and I hit the deck, just in case he was behind me and could see me in the flash. Thunder followed several seconds after.

Although I was glad that the relentless rain might come to an end, I needed it until I figured out where to go.

The building foundations were out of the question. Ranger Johnson would search each one, and it wouldn't take long for him to find me. I cursed, and wished I'd studied the terrain like—

Like Grey. What had she said, the day I told her we'd hidden the diamonds? There was a hollow tree on the north side of the island. It could be a perfect hiding spot.

She hadn't given my any more info than that—and that an old bee's nest was inside it—but it was better than my other options. I was close to that side of the island anyway.

And then the sky opened with stars under the rain.

The flare gun. That was a warning. He was coming for me.

DAY 14

CHRIS'S GOTCHA! ALIVE/TAGGED LIST

~~STEVE~~

D-BAG DEREK

~~ME (CHRIS)~~

~~JACK~~

~~MANNY~~

~~DOUG~~ (left camp)

~~PETE~~

~~HORATIO~~

~~CAM~~

~~JORGE~~

~~RAVI~~

OLLIE

34

Heart pounding, I dragged my bad foot and propelled myself as best as I could. I wished I'd found out more about the tree. How in the great chocolate crickets was I going to find one hollow tree in the middle of at least a thousand?

I had to think of it like a math problem. Eliminate things.

I forced myself to stop and take a breath. To think. Really *think*.

The tree is on the north side of the island. I am on the north side of the island.—Check!

The tree is hollow, and has an "old bee's nest in it."—Hollow trees=*not* the slim birches that I was standing near. I'd need to find a grove of bigger trees.

I closed my eyes, trying to visualize what little I'd seen of the island. The beach was behind me. These narrow-trunked trees stretched out to my left. I decided to go to the right, more northeast. I'd figure out how to spot a hollow tree with a bee's nest in it in the dark in the middle of a downpour once I got there.

The sheets of rain made it nearly impossible to see clearly through my glasses. I had to stop and wipe them every so often, and I made a mental note to invent emergency windshield wipers for my lenses if I got home. I worked my way through the grove by going from tree trunk to tree trunk in an effort to stay as deep in shadow as possible.

The rain glittered around me, and it wasn't from a bolt of lightning: a flashlight.

He was too far away for the beam to reach me, but he was searching the grove and coming over the rise from the beach.

I stopped wiping my glasses and picked up the pace, that barbed boot tightening around my foot. With each step I gritted my teeth and pushed air out of my mouth in a rush. Somewhere in the back of my mind I noticed that my chest was starting to tighten, but the agony in my foot and the fear for my life made asthma take a backseat.

A few steps later, I ducked behind a tree. Flashlight beams pierced the rain behind me, swinging in methodical arcs. My asthma was definitely kicking in.

I took a hit off my inhaler. A fairy fart's worth of medicine came out.

Empty.

I held the cloud as long as possible, and my lungs opened.

I stuck it back in my pocket, just as terrified at being without my meds as I was about being chased for my life. I pounded the tree in frustration. How had I ended up here? Tree bark scratched my hand.

Tree bark scratched my hand!

I stretched out and grabbed a leaf: symmetrical, smooth, pointed ends. Oak! Thank you, tree identification badge!

Now I just had to find the *right* oak tree.

A faint edge of yellow light flashed over the wet leaf in my hand.

Before he found me.

I couldn't turn my own light on—that would be suicide. But I had to find that tree, and fast. My body wanted to run anywhere as fast as my foot would let me, but my brain had to do this more calmly. I didn't have speed, so I had to be smart.

Hollow tree . . . bee's nest. How in the heck would I find that?

It's not that I could tell which trees were hollow by looking at them—or could I? The solution popped into my head like when my dad uncorks champagne on my parents' anniversary.

I hoped I would live to see my parents again.

A hollow tree would be a dead tree—and a dead tree would have no leaves in the middle of July.

And this is where driving rain and glasses became a problem. I shivered and squinted into the dark. There were plenty of trees around me, and I could clearly see their trunks, but the branches, which were waving in the high wind? Not so much.

Another flash from the light. Closer this time. I stepped out from the trunk of safety, and walked to the one directly across from where I was standing. Leaves. Leaves on the ones to the left and right.

More thunder. And the flashlight beams were getting brighter.

Beams? Was Grey helping him?

I set up a system: Take a deep breath, hold it in, cross to the next tree, scan the ones on either side, and so on. I was missing trees in a wider radius, but I couldn't figure out a better approach.

Two trees later, a flashlight beam lit up the tree next to me, swooped to the right, and back to the left. They were turning the lights off while they moved forward, then turned them on every few paces to scan the surroundings. The ranger was way closer than I was comfortable with.

But the light had shown me something important: Three trees away, on my right, was a leafless oak. I just had to cross through the former path of the beam to get to it—and hope that the holder of the flashlight didn't come up on me in the process.

Deep breath.

Hold.

Exhale.

Go.

My foot felt like a dog was tearing it off. I kept looking down, expecting it to be in two pieces. I bit my tongue to stop a groan, focused on where I was going, and motored as fast as I could.

I grabbed the trunk just as I heard "Lights!" shouted over the storm. I dropped to my knees and crouched against the trunk, hoping they weren't looking low. The flashlight opened the night in a yellow wedge. Rain glittered. I put my head down, closed my eyes, and waited, expecting them to see me.

They didn't.

The lights went off.

With a wish, prayer, hope, and appeal that this was the right tree and the opening would be big enough for a kind of pudgy kid from Boston to fit into—I reached up the side of the trunk where I was hiding. No opening. I crouched down, stretched my arms around it, wrapping it in a tight hug, then stood, running my arms from the ground up. The wet bark tore at the skin on the inside of my arms, but there—my right elbow, at about shoulder height sunk in and something wet slapped against me.

I scrambled to that side of the tree.

It was straight out of LeeLee's Winnie-the-Pooh book: a huge oak tree with a hollow knot the size of a car window. The bee's nest stuck out like Pooh's honey pot.

Thank you, Grey, I offered silently.

She'd been right about everything else; I sure hoped her streak was as good as Manny's and this nest was dead. I probably had seconds before those lights came on again, or someone came up to me.

Or before she realized that I might be hiding here.

I reached into the hole with both hands, grabbed the nest, and tried to pull it out.

The fragile paper dissolved to dust in my grip. I cringed, waiting for the attack, but no bees came.

I braced my arms on the edge of the hole, heaved myself up and in.

And immediately started sneezing.

I must've sneezed about twenty times in a row—each time knowing that the lights would click on and I'd be a goner. By the time the sneezing fit had passed, ropes of snot hung from my nose and my sinuses were full and pounding. So was my heart.

The space I was in was barely big enough for me to fit: I twisted around so I faced out, but had to hunch my shoulders, keep my head tucked to my chest, and my legs folded so my knees were at my chin—the ugliest owl on the island. At least it was dry in here.

I got set none too soon, though, as the lights flashed on again. I buried my head, held my breath, and kept my eyes closed tight. I swore I could *feel* the lights on me. They were so bright, they illuminated the inside of my eyelids. My chest burned. I was going to cough. Or gasp. Or do something else that would give me away.

The lights clicked off.

Inside my hiding spot, the sound of the raindrops ran together into a steady, faucet-like gush. There hadn't been any thunder or lightning for a while.

I wondered what time it was. I wondered how long it would take them to find me. I wondered if Chris and Derek had been found, or escaped from the dock. My legs and back ached with the urge to move.

"Lights!" The ranger's voice was so close, I thought he was in front of me. I dropped my chin, closed my eyes, and waited.

It was like an artificial sun. Red spots danced in front of my eyes. They weren't using ordinary flashlights.

"Off!" he called. Back to darkness.

"The kid could be anywhere by now." That voice belonged to Ranger Johnson. Voices carry more at night, but I would have bet my life they were next to my tree. *The tree that Grey knew about.* "Let's find the diamonds before he gets 'em and get outta here so we can end this."

Did they really think I was after the diamonds instead of hiding to save my skin? If this was one of those Choose Your Own Adventure novels I read in fifth grade, I'd have picked wrong already: "Climb into the hollow tree to hide—go to page 47. Retrieve the diamonds from the hiding place and use them to barter your freedom—go to page 89." Page 47 would read, "You are trapped and you die. Try again."

"No," said Grey. Not "No—he's my friend," not "No—I don't know where they are," just "No." She didn't care about me—not one bit. And here I'd been worried about *her* safety! I seethed.

Despite my sopping-wet, freezing clothes, sweat broke out all over my body. I shivered, which kicked up more bee's nest dust.

My nose prickled.

I was going to sneeze again.

35

I did every trick I could think of—sniffing, holding my breath, rubbing my nose—but it was no use.

I sneezed. Loudly.

I held my breath again and closed my eyes. Waited. Hoped.

The lights came on and this time it was like sunshine bathing my face. I opened my eyes and squinted into the downpour. The flashlights blinded me, and the rain sparkled through the beams.

"Ugliest owl on the island," Ranger Johnson growled. "Get out."

I wriggled so I could grab the edge of the hole and push myself out. Unfortunately, my bunched-up legs had gone numb, and I fell, flat on my face. I barely had enough time to get my hands out in front so I wouldn't break my nose, but I still got a mouthful of mud.

The lights never wavered. I wiped my mouth and spit.

"Get up." The ranger spoke sharply.

I tried, but my now-tingling legs were slow to cooperate. The rain pelted down, making me even colder than I was before, if that was possible. The tree had been warmer than I'd realized.

Ranger Johnson's big hand clasped around my upper arm with way more force than necessary. He pulled me to my feet the way my mom did with LeeLee when she was having a tantrum in the PlaySpace at the mall.

I still couldn't feel anything below my knees, but I managed to stand straight.

"Take us to the diamonds. Now," he ordered. Grey stood beside him, stone faced.

There was no SWAT team to save me. No way for me to send a message for help. I was on my own this time.

So I obeyed.

When I stepped forward on my bad foot, though, I nearly screamed. The pain was unbelievable. I was pretty sure I hadn't broken a bone, but whatever snapped in there was critical for things that feet do. Walking, especially.

There was no way I could walk across the island like this.

"I hurt my foot," I said in a raspy whisper. I cleared my throat and tried again. "I hurt my foot. I can't walk far. I can tell you where the diamonds are . . ."

"You have to walk," he commanded. "We need the diamonds by sunrise."

I stepped again, this time with my good foot, and kind of dragged the bad one behind it. The pain was still white-hot with each movement, but bearable.

Slowly, I limped through the grove, heading back to the foundations.

Grey and her dad held their lights out, illuminating my path.

Water rushed down the little hills between the trees. I couldn't believe it had been raining this hard, for this long.

I couldn't believe I was leading these jerks to the diamonds either.

LATER THAT NIGHT
36

A slow, painful walk later, we reached the foundation of the big building where Chris and I stashed the diamonds. Ranger Johnson and Grey hadn't spoken to me at all, other than to tell me to move faster.

That scared me even more.

"Here," I said. I'd long ago lost track of what time it was, but that didn't matter. This was the longest night in history and I was seriously doubting I'd get to see sunrise.

"Go get them," the ranger said.

I remembered the slick stairs, even on a day when there hadn't been rain in over a week. And the steel bars sticking out of the foundation. And the goop on the ground. And the basketball-sized bruise on my back and butt from the previous trip. My chest tightened at the thought.

"I don't think that's the best idea," I replied. I coughed, trying to open my airways.

"Go."

"Just do what he says," Grey spoke up. "Get them, bring them back, and we're done. If you and Chris hadn't moved them, we wouldn't even be here right now."

Cold steel pushed against the spot between my shoulder blades. The flare gun. My breath hitched again, lungs shrinking. I wheezed.

And moved.

One slow step at a time, I dragged myself to the edge of the foundation near the stairs. I flashed back to Chris and me treading carefully along the perimeter—and that was with two good feet.

My lungs were the size of oranges. I tried to keep my breath even and focus tight. They held the lights steady on the foundation. The shadows were deep, and it was nearly impossible to see the bottom between the shadows and the rain.

And that was when I realized: There might be a way out of this yet.

I took short, slow breaths like my asthma doc taught me, and limped to the edge of the foundation. I had to climb up on my hands and knees, which thankfully lessened the pain in my foot.

Crawling along the edge of the foundation, the stone slippery and cold under my hands, I inched to the staircase. The painful choices: Stand or go down on my butt. But for even a teeny chance of making this work, I'd have to walk down the stairs.

I took as deep a breath as my tortured lungs would let me, clenched my jaw, and stood. A silver streak shot up my leg from my foot, but I could handle it. One step: good foot, bad foot. Next step: good foot, bad foot. And the next. And the next. I kept one hand against the rain-slicked wall for balance.

The farther I went, the more my heart pounded. Four steps from the bottom, I spotted the collection of wet leaves and rabbit poop that piled up on the last few risers that caused my fall last time.

"That's it," called Ranger Johnson. Was he trying to be *encouraging?* "Keep going."

"Trying," I wheezed. The most important thing was to not let them see me change my approach for the last few steps. The wet pile was hard to see from ground level. I leaned a little more toward the wall and made sure to plant my feet squarely in the muck—but I didn't try to scrape any of it off.

Three more . . . two more . . . one . . . and *down*. Level ground.

As fast as I dared, I limped across the room, trying to stick to the middle of the floor and the light from the flashlights. My chest was still tight, but the asthma attack hadn't gotten any worse. I needed to hold out a little longer.

Hoping I got the topography of the room correct, I made a sharp turn to the right and into an alcove, deep in shadow—shadows that were at a funny angle for the flashlights to penetrate.

"Ollie! You got the bag?" That was Grey.

I stayed silent.

"Ollie!" she called again. One of the lights winked off.

I expected this. The ranger would send Grey around the foundation, estimating where I was standing, and she'd turn her light on again. While she was on her way over, I crossed to the far side of the foundation, into another alcove—closer to the stairs and Ranger Johnson. Although I couldn't do this for the rest of the night, I hoped it would buy me time.

Across the way, the bright light clicked on, revealing only the empty space. Immediately, the light swung left and right: She assumed she went to the wrong alcove.

"He's not here," she said. How had I ever thought this girl was "interesting"? She was scary.

"Of course he's here," the ranger replied, putting calm cucumbers to shame. "We just need to find him."

The real Gotcha! game was well under way.

A beam reflected off the rain. Ranger Johnson. Grey would have taken longer to go back around to the staircase. My lungs tightened up to lemon-sized. I crouched and took harsh breaths through my mouth, grateful for the continuous, icy, noisy, pounding rain.

Ranger Johnson's light was staying too steady. He knew the islands perfectly, and wanted those diamonds to get someone off his—and Grey's—back. My only hope was that—

And then it happened. A jittery, jouncing blade of light, a shout, and groan. Yeah, wet leaves! I hoped his butt and back hurt as much as mine had.

"Dad!" Grey shouted. "Are you okay?"

Another groan.

"Grey, I can't get up. Something snapped in my leg." Another groan from Ranger Johnson. I almost felt bad for him. Almost.

I'd stayed away from the approximate area where Chris and I left the pillowcase. Even though there was no way for me to

259

win this, I really, really didn't want to give up the diamonds. Especially not to them. What had happened? Who did Ranger Johnson need to give them to? Why was Grey being threatened?

Grey's light went off.

Things had been quiet for too long. *Someone* needed to come down here. Or get me from the top.

My heart whomped: *whomp-whomp-whomp.*

And stronger, shaking my whole chest: *Whomp. Whomp. Whomp.*

That wasn't just my heart.

That was a helicopter.

37

Eyes to the sky, I strained to see it. The sound of the rotors grew louder, and then, from above, came a bright searchlight. It swooped over the foundation, and I had a second to decide: Wave and reveal my location to everyone, or duck deeper into the shadows and hope that the people on the copter would try to rescue me?

If they were, in fact, rescuers—and not the guys that Ranger Johnson had been talking about.

That did it. I scrabbled under an outcropping of rock and mortar and pressed myself as tight against it as I could. The lights slid over me; I hoped I hadn't been spotted.

"Over here!" yelled Ranger Johnson. I wanted to shake my head. Did the guy have any idea how dangerous that was?

My lungs were the size of limes. I coughed, hard, and gripped my empty inhaler. I longed to use it, but I needed to save whatever wisps of medicine remained for when the attack got *really, really* bad.

Not just *really* bad.

The helicopter circled away. They'd have to land on the open part of the island—on the exact opposite side from where we were.

Grey kept her light off.

"Grey! Honey! Are you there? Don't leave!" His voice cracked. "Don't leave me!"

"I'm here!" she yelled.

I came out from my shabby hiding spot and sat, back against the wall, trying to think, breathe, and not freeze to death.

Even though she had betrayed me, I still had a shred of concern for Grey. Some guys had threatened her, and the ranger needed to keep her safe by giving them the diamonds? Was there a way I could save her, the diamonds, and myself?

Did I want to?

Maybe.

I stood, hissing through clenched teeth as I did so, and slowly made my way across the foundation, toward the diamonds. Every step hurt: my foot, my lungs, my back. This was it, and if it didn't work, I was out of options.

I tried to muffle my coughs, but each breath was a fight. I'd reached the spot where I thought we left the pillowcase, but it wasn't there. A frantic few seconds followed before I realized that I was off by a few feet. Then I spotted the rock pile.

Carefully, I moved the rocks. Found the pillowcase. Dumped out the diamonds.

Quickly, I grabbed some rocks about the same size and tossed them in. I kept one of the dirty diamonds and stuck it in my pocket. Then I twisted up the neck of the pillowcase and wrapped it around my wrist.

I made the long, slow trek back to the stairs. The rain had eased and I could see a little. My chest ached.

Ranger Johnson was still in a heap on the floor. Even in

the dark, I could see his face: white and twisted with pain.

"If I don't give them money, they'll take Grey. I just want to keep her safe." Tears mixed with rain ran down his cheeks.

I just coughed. I had one shout in me, and it was going to her.

I brought out my inhaler and tried to get the tiniest bit of medicine that was left. My lungs went back to the size of oranges.

"Grey! I have the diamonds!" I yelled as loud as I could. Just once.

Then waited.

It was eternity.

Each breath squeezed into my lungs like I was sucking it through a coffee stirrer.

Then: light. Blinding, harsh, and exactly the same as before. Grey.

"Bring them up, Ollie."

I shook my head. I couldn't get up the stairs. Not with my foot, not with my asthma, not for anything—or anyone. Especially not Grey.

I held up the pillowcase and coughed some more.

"He's got them!" Ranger Johnson, trying to be helpful. "The pillowcase is exactly what you described. Take it back to the tree, hon. Fast."

I leaned against the wall at the foot of the stairs, trying to inhale. *Heeze! Heeze! Heeze!* went my chest. My breathing was finally louder than the rain.

"Throw it," Grey commanded.

My hands shook, and I fought against the panic that rose like the tide as I tried to get air. I was *not* going to choke to death. I forced myself to go slowly; knotted the pillowcase so nothing would fall out.

I swung it around a couple of times, let it get momentum. Tossed it up and out of the foundation, onto the ground. Then I sagged against the dripping wall, my chest constricting tighter and tighter.

Grey's light disappeared.

"Got 'em!" she screamed. "But they're all the filthy ones! Daddy, they'll think they're just rocks. The tin is at home!" Even shouting, I could hear the fear in her voice.

I shook my head, raised my hand.

"Ollie's shaking his head!" yelled Ranger Johnson. "Wait a second!"

I reached into my pocket and removed the Death Star pencil sharpener, held it up. I seriously did not know how much longer I would stay conscious, I was wheezing and choking so much.

"He's got something!" shouted Johnson. I tossed the pencil sharpener. My aim wasn't great this time. Hopefully Grey could figure out how to open the Death Star.

I sank to my knees, my forehead on the step.

"Got it!" she yelled. "Thanks, Ollie."

"Go!" Ranger Johnson screamed. "Quick! Go!"

Her light clicked off, and Ranger Johnson and I were left in darkness.

My vision had narrowed to pinpricks, and I couldn't tell if the darkness was from the night sky or the beginnings of loss of consciousness. My hands tingled and my feet were balloons. At least I couldn't feel the rain anymore.

Another light stabbed down into the foundation. Shouting. Guys in white.

The Coast Guard made it across the island—finally.

Ranger Johnson yelled, and then there was a warm hand on my back. I tried to talk, but all that came out was *Eee! Eee! Eee!*

Then, a stinging pinch in my thigh.

And, an eternity later—an oxygen mask. Cool, fresh, menthol-tasting oxygen. I closed my eyes; inhaled. My raw throat opened a little. My lungs expanded a little more.

"Take it easy, buddy. Take it slow."

I gasped, pushed the mask away, pointed to where Ranger Johnson was being tended to by other guys.

"It's him," I gasped. "He started it."

CHRIS'S GOTCHA! ALIVE/TAGGED LIST

~~STEVE~~

D-BAG DEREK

~~ME (CHRIS)~~

~~JACK~~

~~MANNY~~

~~DOUG~~ (left camp)

~~PETE~~

~~HORATIO~~

~~CAM~~

~~JORGE~~

~~RAVI~~

OLLIE

THE AFTERMATH

Here's how getting out of trouble looks:

Me, strapped to a stretcher, soaking wet, shivering, barely able to breathe, and in a ton of pain.

Grey ran up to me while I was parked at the edge of the grass, waiting while they loaded Ranger Johnson into the copter first. I'd seen her go over to him, watched as his shoulders sagged with relief, watched their hug. Behind them, the sun was rising, streaking the sky pink and gold. No more rain.

Then she raced across the field, wrapped in a dark blanket, wet hair hanging in clumps.

"Are you okay?" She was out of breath when she got to me.

I slid the mask out of the way. "Yeah. Just the asthma. And my foot. And the trauma of being kidnapped, chased, and threatened. You?"

"Fine. Look, I'm sorry, Ollie. I had to do it. My dad owed these guys lots of money. It was the diamonds or me."

I shrugged. "Yeah. Whatever."

That's when she leaned over and pressed her lips to mine. Her hair dripped on to my face. I didn't kiss her back.

"Yeah, whatever," she said after she pulled away.

I wanted to wipe my mouth and spit, but I settled for scowling at her.

"Thanks," she said.

A Coast Guard officer came over.

They loaded me onto the copter.

It wasn't until I was in my hospital bed, until Agent Goh came in, that I told anyone the truth. That the diamonds were still on the ground in the foundation. That I'd given Grey—and whoever picked up the pillowcase—just some old rocks. That I had coordinates and everything.

"Impressive, Ollie." Agent Goh sat at the bottom of my bed, near my bad foot. I'd torn a tendon in it—nothing serious, but I'd have to wear a boot for six weeks and go to physical therapy. "But I'm not surprised. You're getting good at this stuff."

He told me that Ranger Johnson had a problem—a gambling problem. He bet on horses, the Sox, the Celtics—any sport he could. He owed some bad people a lot of money, and then he tried to cover it all by betting on a Sox game. And that's when the guys started threatening Grey.

"We're putting them in protective custody," Agent Goh said. "Ranger Johnson has agreed to help us with the investigation. And now that we know that his bookies only have plain rocks, he, Grey, and her mom will be in a lot more danger."

"But they'll be safe with you guys?"

"They'll be safe. And although you might be good at this, you need to stay out of trouble like we talked about," Agent Goh finished.

He barely got the words out when Chris, Manny and . . . Derek?! all came to the door. I waved them in.

"Hey Ollie," Chris said. "You look good, I mean, not really, but better than I thought you would after everything. Did you know Manny rescued us? He never broke his streak, and came out for a swim and saw—hey, who're you? Ollie's uncle or something?"

Agent Goh raised an eyebrow at me.

"Um, yeah. Uncle . . ." I trailed off. "This is Chris, and Manny. And, uh, Derek."

Chris crowded close to me and pressed something into my hand. I didn't look down, just closed my fist around it.

"We wanted to make sure you were okay and stuff. And see what was going to happen to the diamonds." He looked hopeful.

"The Pirate Museum in Salem will get them for authentication," I answered. "Then the Parks Service, the Coast Guard, and the FBI have to figure out where they'll go permanently, I guess. But I told everyone that you helped find them." Agent Goh stood to leave.

"Thanks for everything . . . Uncle," I told him. He nodded.

"Hey Sherlock, Mr. Fuentes wanted me to tell you that you're not provo anymore," Derek said. A big bandage—from his fall on the dock—covered his temple. "You're an honorary member of Troop Seven." He held out a Troop 7 patch.

"Thanks, D," I said, enjoying the promotion. I leaned over to take the patch from him, but planted the red sticker, care of Chris, on his arm, instead.

"Gotcha!"

(Target/Path)

CHRIS'S GOTCHA! ~~ALIVE/TAGGED~~ LIST

~~STEVE~~   Jack →Ravi (takes himself out
                        to avoid tagging Ravi)

~~D-BAG DEREK~~   Cam

~~ME (CHRIS)~~   Doug (leaves camp)

~~JACK~~   Ravi

~~MANNY~~   Steve

~~DOUG~~ (left camp)   Jorge → Ollie

~~PETE~~   Manny

~~HORATIO~~   Chris

~~CAM~~   Horatio → Chris →Doug→Ollie

~~JORGE~~   Ollie

~~RAVI~~   Derek

~~OLLIE~~   Pete →Manny
                    ↳ Steve (Takes himself out)
                      ↳Ravi →Derek

AUTHOR'S NOTE

The Boston Harbor Islands are real places, open to visitors, and are filled with secrets and lore. I stayed true to their names and stories, but took liberties with their topography. To find out more about these parks, visit www.bostonharborislands.org.

- For information about George's Island Lady in Black, visit:www.celebrateboston.com /ghost/georges-island-lady-in-black-ghost.htm
- To read the text of the letter Capt. Kidd left outlining where his treasure lies on Conant's Island, check out Under the Connecticut River: www.bio.umass .edu/biology/conn.river/palmer.html
- To learn about Long Ben Avery's piracy and treasure, go to www.captainkidd.org/john%20Avery.html
- The Pirate Museum in Salem, Massachusetts, is home to all things New England pirate: www.piratemuseum.com/pirate.html

- Interested in geocaching? www.geocaching.com should be your first stop.
- My Wilderness Scouts are a fictional creation. For information on the official Wilderness Scouts, visit wilderness-scouts.org

ACKNOWLEDGMENTS

LIZ WANIEWSKI, editor — So patient, excellent suggestions; her tenacity made this book take shape

SALLY HARDING, agent — Cheerleader, supporter extraordinaire

REGINA CASTILLO, copyeditor — Points out and helps fix my mistakes—any left are mine alone

LINDSAY BOGGS, publicist — Gets the word out about the books

JASMIN RUBERO and TONY SAHARA, designers — Make the book look great

ANNETTE, GARY, HEATHER, KATE, MEGAN, PHOEBE—critique group — Suffers through early drafts, patiently critiques and comments on each revision

BOB STYMEIST—bird/wildlife census info — Helped me get that part right (liberties are mine, accuracies his)

CHRIS I., Troop 7, West Roxbury	Lent his name (and a few attributes) to the story
TROOP 7, West Roxbury	Model for the Wilderness Scouts
JOSH DOUGHERTY, Troop 28	Reader, expert in all things scouting, and twelve-year-old boy
KRISTEN CAPPY, Curious City	Provides promotion and support for the books, helps them reach their audience
PANACHE COFFEE	Provides quiet writing space, copious amounts of iced tea and cookies

FRANK, husband

Maintains all aspects of the household and child care during the writing process, supports me unconditionally

MY KIDS

Put up with Mommy's late nights, fractured days, and disappearances—and who hug me so tight when I come home

ABOUT THE AUTHOR

Erin Dionne is the author of fresh, funny, and foible-filled books for middle grade readers, including *Models Don't Eat Chocolate Cookies*, *The Total Tragedy of a Girl Named Hamlet*, *Notes from an Accidental Band Geek*, and *Moxie and the Art of Rule Breaking*. She lives outside of Boston with her husband, two children, and dog, and teaches at Montserrat College of Art. She has only slept in a tent once, and is totally fine with that. When she's not writing, teaching, or being a mom, she loves talking to book groups, libraries and classes about reading and writing. Find her online at www.erindionne.com.